THE MOUNTAIN PARADOX

MARGARET EMERSON

THE MOUNTAIN PARADOX

CURIOUS STORIES SET IN A SMALL TOWN IN SOUTHWEST COLORADO

Images and Adjectives Publishing, LLC

ISBN: 978-0-578-37208-2

This is a work of fiction. Names, characters, events and incidents are the products of the author's imagination. Any resemblance to actual persons, living or dead, or actual events is purely coincidental.

Front cover image © Kwiktor | Dreamstime.com / 128301257
Book design by Margaret Emerson
Printed in the United States of America.
First printing edition 2022.

Images and Adjectives Publishing, LLC
2119 County Road 1A
Montrose, CO 81403
www.RidgwayWritingWorkshops.com

DEDICATION

*For David. Thank you for being my steadfast partner
on this amazing adventure.*

CONTENTS

MISSING

"Until you make the unconscious conscious, it will direct your life and you will call it fate."
— C.G. Jung

Charlie looked at his phone. Judy had been gone since about three that afternoon. She had popped her head into his office before she left and said she was going to the grocery store in Montrose, a 30-minute drive south.

It was now almost 6:30.

He texted her and then ambled to the kitchen to see what there was to eat in the refrigerator.

Are you on your way home?

What could be taking her so long to get groceries? Maybe she had other errands. Maybe she had a hair appointment and didn't mention it.

He picked up the Glad plastic containers in the refrigerator and remembered the meal they had the night before, and the night before that. Lasagna. Beef teriyaki. He reached in farther back and found a smaller container that looked like it contained oatmeal with dark blue blotches. Blueberries? Mold? It must have been Judy's leftovers because he didn't like oatmeal.

He grabbed the container with the lasagna and a can of beer, put the lasagna in the microwave and then pulled the tab on the can and savored the crack-hiss for a second before taking a sip.

He looked at his phone again. No response yet from Judy. Maybe she was driving. He opened the Find My Phone app and waited for it to pinpoint her location.

The microwave beeped. He put his phone down on the kitchen counter and retrieved the heated tub of leftover vegetarian lasagna. It was very hot, and he almost dropped it, but managed to set it down before it burned his fingers. He slid the tub onto a plate, got a fork and sat down at the counter where he'd left his phone.

He looked at the phone screen to see what the app indicated.

Judy's iPhone
Montrose, CO · Today at 3:47 PM

He clicked on the report and the map above it shifted to a dot in the middle of a green area with a road. He zoomed out. A gray dot appeared on the map above the report. He zoomed in to gain context of the location. The dot sat frozen on highway 90, at least several miles west of Montrose, surrounded by a green area without any other roads or streets. When he zoomed out, the dot didn't move. It remained far west of the grocery store and shopping area where he expected her to have been.

"What in the heck?"

Where had she gone? They didn't know anyone who lived west of Montrose. And there were no stores or houses that far west near the National Forest boundary. Even more odd was that the phone pinged her location there at 3:47 PM, which meant she hadn't even gone to the grocery store; she'd driven straight to that location.

He pulled up the phone app, navigated to the "recents" menu and touched her name on the list. After a few rings, he heard her voicemail recording.

Hi, this is Judy. Please leave a message and I'll get back to you soon.

Charlie cleared his throat. "Hey, where are you? Give me a call as soon as you get this. It's about 6:30 and I was expecting you'd be home by now."

He checked the calendar app since his and Judy's Apple ID were the same and she put all her appointments and to-do reminders there. He scrolled up and down on the day. There were no entries.

He looked up and stared at the kitchen cabinets, chewing the noodles and sauce without pleasure.

Should he call Judy's friend, Barb? Maybe Barb knew where Judy might have been going. But he didn't want to alarm her, yet. Instead, he found the number to the county sheriff on his contact list and pressed the entry. It rang four times before someone picked up.

"Hi, yes, this is Charlie Davenport calling from Log Hill? Um, I'm calling because I can't reach my wife, who's been gone four hours and past due from going grocery shopping in Montrose. I'm wondering if there were any accidents reported on highway 550?" Charlie thought for a second. "Or anywhere in Montrose?"

The man who answered the phone put him on hold.

Charlie felt heat rising to his face and his hand started to shake. He looked at his phone screen again, checked to make sure silent mode was toggled off, and put the phone back up to his ear.

"Sir? Yes, there were no accidents reported this afternoon in Ouray county. Not sure about Montrose county. You may want to call the Montrose county sheriff for that information."

"Oh, ok. I will."

Charlie hung up and looked up the next phone number to connect to.

A few minutes later, after speaking to a woman and then a man, he was back where he started with no more new information. There were no accidents reported that day.

He ate a few more bites while he deliberated what to do next. Most likely there was a logical, reasonable explanation for where she was and why she wasn't home yet. Maybe Judy had been contacted by a friend who needed help on her way into town and was on her way to meet her. There were some hiking trails in the National Forest area west of Montrose that Judy had explored in the past with Barb and her other hiking friends. Charlie wasn't familiar with those trails, however, since he hadn't gone hiking all year due to his knee issues.

Ever since he retired, his physical stamina and abilities had really suffered. Two years ago he had to have back surgery and could only do easy, steady walks for exercise. This year his back was feeling better, but an old ski injury was giving him knee pain.

Judy, on the other hand, was very fit and hiked at least twice a week after they moved to Ridgway.

Did she decide to go hiking out of the blue in the middle of the day? That wasn't like her. She didn't like going hiking this late in the day. She was a morning lark and liked to get her hikes done by mid-afternoon, before her energy waned.

She wouldn't have gone by herself, would she? She didn't typically do that, either, unless it was at the state park or somewhere close by.

Charlie checked the Find My Phone app again, and this time it said *No Location Found* under "Judy's iPhone".

Something didn't sit right with this situation. Maybe she had gone looking for something and her car broke down. He pondered his options. Not wanting to waste any more daylight hours, he scribbled a short note and left it on the kitchen counter where

Judy would see it in case she got home before he did. Then he got his keys and made his way to the garage and his pickup truck.

*

An hour later, he was past the area where Judy's cellphone stopped pinging her location along highway 90. Not knowing exactly where she lost cell service, he drove well under the speed limit and looked around at both sides of the road in case her white Subaru Outback had skidded off into the trees or was parked to the side. The sun was close to the western horizon and the skies were clear. It had been a bluebird day, with temperatures in the upper 70s on the mesa and ten degrees hotter lower down in town.

Shortly after seeing the "Entering the Uncompahgre National Forest" sign, he lost cell service on his phone. He was glad he'd called Barb while he was still within the service area to ask her if she knew anything about Judy's whereabouts. She didn't. She hadn't heard from Judy at all today and had no idea where she might be, but she said she'd ask their group of friends to see if anyone had heard from her.

He turned north on Divide Road, a relatively narrow dirt road that cut through a thick forest of spruce and pine and ended almost 100 miles north in the scrubby desert near Grand Junction. He slowed down to inspect several side roads that were more like driveways leading to muddy, rutted clearings. No white Subarus. He spotted a few groups boondocking with campers and travel trailers, but for the most part, this part of the Uncompahgre Plateau was sparsely populated. In the fall, this was a popular spot for elk hunting. In the winter, families bought permits to select and cut a Christmas tree. But in the summer, it was mostly visited by campers, four-wheelers, mountain bikers, and hikers.

He slowed down to see if he could spot her car at the two small National Forest campgrounds he passed. He wasn't sure if he should turn and check out the service roads that intersected or stick to the main road, so he chose the latter. The sun was low and likely already below the horizon but there was still enough light to see a short distance into the woods and down side roads. Charlie disliked driving at this time of the day because deer were actively on the move and hard to see in the low contrast of dusk. He had to be vigilant to avoid hitting the ones that crossed the road.

He checked his phone and saw that it was 8:14 PM and he still didn't have service. If he turned around now, he could be home by 9:45 or so, and for sure if Judy was out doing something with a friend, she would be home and waiting for him by then. They were usually in bed by nine.

A half an hour later, he was making his way down another road that led back to Montrose, looking down at the street and house lights twinkling in the valley, and his phone pinged. It was Barb, asking if he'd heard anything yet and letting him know no one she spoke to had heard from Judy today.

He tried calling Judy again and let out a long, labored sigh when he heard her voicemail greeting after several seconds of silence. She must have still been out of range.

*

Charlie didn't get to bed until past 2 AM.

Judy hadn't been home when he got back, so he called the sheriff again.

A short time later, the sheriff arrived, and Charlie led him inside the house, where they sat down at the kitchen table. He made a few calls, one of which was to inquire if any hospitals in the area had admitted her or someone matching her description:

a petite woman, age 65, short blonde hair and average weight. He then took Charlie's statement and asked questions about his whereabouts that day, Judy's typical routine and possible places she may have gone. He didn't dismiss Charlie's assertion that she had mysteriously driven north and west, but he told Charlie that sometimes tracking apps were unreliable for pinpointing a person's last known location.

Charlie told the sheriff he had driven up there anyway, to see if he could find her in case her car broke down, or if she had gone hiking—although he wasn't sure where the trails were up there.

The sheriff told Charlie he'd contact both the Montrose county sheriff and the San Miguel county sheriff and put out an inter-agency alert for a missing person. They'd send out someone to check the popular trailheads on the plateau to see if they could find her car.

"Hopefully she'll call you soon," the sheriff said as he got up to leave. "Maybe this was all a big misunderstanding. I recommend checking with your credit card issuer to see if she's made any purchases today. Or if she took out any cash at the bank. Mean-while, I'll make some inquiries and I'll be in touch with you in the morning."

"Thanks sheriff. I'll do the same if I hear anything."

Charlie went online to check their credit card and bank state-ments. Other than an automatic, recurring charge for trash ser-vice, no other charges were made on their bank cards that day. Not to the grocery store, not to a gas station. Nothing.

He checked the closet to see if her daypack and hiking boots were still there. They were. So was her water bottle, half-full of water and tucked into the side pocket of her daypack from the last time she'd used it.

It's as if she had left with the intention of getting groceries, gotten sidetracked by something or someone, and couldn't get back home for some reason.

But what was that reason? Charlie lay awake, reviewing all the possibilities, occasionally getting up to Google something, until the first light of day shone through the uncovered bedroom windows.

*

"What was the last thing she said to you?" asked Barb. She and Kathy—another of Judy's friends—had come by the next morning to see what they could do to help with the search for Judy. He had offered them some coffee and they sat around the kitchen table, brainstorming.

"Just that she was going to get groceries and did I need anything from the store."

"What about before that? Earlier. Did she say anything?"

Charlie couldn't recall anything unusual that she might have said. He had spent the morning going over some paperwork he'd gotten from one of the environmental organizations for which he was a volunteer. In the afternoon he took a walk and then was in his office replying to emails while Judy was doing something in the living room and in the kitchen (*what had she been doing? No food had been prepared that he could see.*)

He'd been an environmental issues attorney before he retired, and Judy worked in human resources the last ten years before they had moved to Ridgway. They both lived in Riverside, California but decided they wanted to retire to Colorado because they loved the mountains and fresh air and had vacationed in Ridgway and Ouray many summers.

Their daughter and son were both in their 30s and still living in the Los Angeles area. Charlie called them earlier that morning and shared the news that their mother was missing. Their daughter, Melissa, said she was going to book a flight to Montrose and get there as soon as she could to help in the search. Jack couldn't leave right away but planned on driving to Colorado in the next few days, and made himself available for any tasks or research in the meantime.

"Have you checked to see if she'd had any appointments, maybe? Maybe she was going to meet someone from Craigslist. You know how much she liked to buy and sell on Craigslist," said Kathy, a lanky woman with short, salt and pepper hair and a baritone voice. Charlie didn't care for Kathy. He always thought she was abrasive and condescending. She'd make snide comments about the books he had on the coffee table when she'd come by to visit Judy.

"Why are you reading a biography of that asshat? I can't stand that guy."

"I'm surprised you're into self-help. I didn't think men had an interest in self-improvement."

Or she'd make remarks about his clothes.

"Hey Charlie? The 80s called. They want their jacket back."

She'd always laugh at her own remarks, as if that would take the sting out of it. As if it was too late to take it back, so she had to put a verbal band-aid on what came out of her mouth.

"I don't think she was selling or buying anything on Craigslist yesterday, Kathy." Charlie's lips pressed together before he took another sip of coffee.

"Do you have her passwords? Maybe we can check her email," Barb suggested.

"Yeah, I was going to do that. Hopefully her laptop isn't password protected," Charlie said as closed his eyes, trying to visualize if he'd ever seen Judy typing into a password field before using it. "I do think I know where she kept a list of passwords."

As Charlie rose out of his chair, he felt the weight of the last twelve hours slump heavily on him. The sleepless night was like a 100-pound backpack strapped to his back, his head tingled, and his legs were leaden. The coffee wasn't making a dent. He wished Kathy and Barb would go home so he could go lie down.

He found the little notebook with Judy's passwords on a counter of their large kitchen, in an organizer that had trays of receipts, unopened mail, unpaid bills and a few printouts of recipes. He grabbed it and was returning to the table where the women were whispering to each other when his phone rang. It was a local number. Charlie answered immediately.

"Yeah?"

"Hi Mr. Davenport, this is Sheriff Turner. I wanted to call and update you on a few things about your missing wife."

"Okay."

"We checked all of the hiking trailheads in that five mile stretch of the plateau where you think she may have gone, but we didn't see any cars there."

"Oh."

"We put out a call on her license plate in case any of our deputies see her car. We contacted Montrose county, Mesa county, San Miguel, even San Juan and Dolores in case she went that far. They're keeping an eye out," the sheriff reported. He paused, and Charlie heard him shuffling papers. "Were you able to look at bank and credit card transactions?"

"I did, last night. Nothing yesterday, unfortunately."

"What about this morning?"

"I haven't had a chance to check again."

"Okay, I advise you do that as soon as you can. Have you been in contact with her friends and family?"

"Yes, I called our kids, and her two good friends are here right now. They don't know anything."

"I see. Alright, I've got a few things I'm going to be checking into and I'll be in touch later today."

Charlie hung up and put the phone down on the kitchen table along with the little purple notebook.

"Charlie," Barb looked directly at him with her kind, blue eyes. "We were just talking about how we think that Judy had been acting not herself lately. Had you noticed that?"

"What do you mean?"

"Oh, she seemed—distracted somehow. A little more subdued. Actually, she had canceled plans a couple of times recently without a real explanation as to why." Barb's expression appeared to be asking Charlie to explain.

"I don't know, Barb. She hadn't said anything to me," Charlie said. "How long ago did you notice this about her?"

"Oh, I don't know. Maybe a few months? What do you think, Kathy?"

Kathy sat erect, leering at Charlie.

"Yeah, I'd say since spring? So yeah, a few months." She looked down at her empty coffee cup. "Listen, Barb, we should probably go. Maybe someone in town will have seen her or heard something. We'll make some calls." She stood up and pushed her chair back under the table. "I'm sure Charlie can't wait to get us out of his hair. He looks like hell."

Ignoring the reference to his appearance, he stood up and started walking to the sink with his mug. "Thanks for coming by, ladies. I'll let you know if—what I find out."

He let them leave without bothering to walk them to the front door, waited a few minutes, and then sat back down at the kitchen table. He opened the little notebook and started flipping through the pages filled with Judy's neat, steady handwriting.

Judy had a Gmail account. The login was one of the entries on the last two pages in the notebook, indicating to him that it was a more recent entry. Satisfied that he'd be able to check her email from his own laptop, he got up and lumbered to the bedroom, where he fell into bed and into a fitful, but needed, sleep.

*

Melissa arrived at Montrose on the last flight to the small airport that night. Charlie got there early enough to park and go inside to meet her in the terminal. When she emerged from behind baggage claim and made eye contact, she ran to him, let go of her carry on, and they fell into a long, tight embrace. Charlie felt a deep well of emotion lift up out of his chest and began sobbing on her shoulder.

"Oh dad, I'm so sorry. I'm so sorry," Melissa said. Charlie stepped back and rubbed his face with the back of his hand. Melissa's eyes were red-rimmed and puffy and her eyebrows arched into an expression of concern and compassion.

"I'm sorry, too, kiddo. I was hoping to have good news before you got here."

"So still nothing?"

"Nothing," Charlie croaked. "Her car hasn't been found and there still haven't been any charges on the cards. Our neighbor Tim has offered to get a couple guys to go with him tomorrow with some ATVs and search the plateau off Divide Road to see if they can find her car. I mean, it's miles of side and forest service roads up there, most of them impassable with a car. Or even my truck. I spent a couple hours up there today and got turned around a few times."

"I wouldn't want you going up there by yourself, anyway, Dad. The last thing we need is for you to get stuck in the middle of nowhere or get lost yourself," Melissa said.

Once they were out of the airport and on the road headed south, Melissa turned her head to look out the window to the west, where the sky was magenta and purple and streaked in high, thin clouds. In the shadow of sunset, the valley rose gradually up to the edge of the plateau, 40 miles away, a black shape that spanned from the 10,000-foot-high Horsefly Peak to the mostly-sage desert canyons that descended to 4,500 feet at the town of Grand Junction. "I guess it's a good thing it's not that cold out, in case she's had to spend a night or two in her car. But why did she even go up there?"

"It seems like the most reasonable explanation is that she decided to do a hike up there for some reason by herself. Which is really unlike her. I just don't know what else could have happened. No one's heard from her."

"Do you think it's possible she was carjacked or kidnapped?"

Charlie had considered that possibility already, but it seemed so unlikely. Judy was in her 60s, not really a candidate for human trafficking, which had become rampant in rural areas of the west. Men would lure young women in parking lots or gas stations, and they'd be drugged before being put in a van and driven to where they'd be kept for the commercial sex trade. Mostly, this was a crime performed on immigrants or women from very poor areas. Not on retired, middle-class women from affluent towns like Ridgway.

He even wondered if someone carjacked her in order to rob her and take her car. Maybe leaving her on the side of the road to find her way back to town. But Judy rarely carried much cash, and her car was an older model and not worth that much money.

No, he didn't even want to consider the possibility that a psychopath had kidnapped her with the intent to torture and kill her. From where would this person have kidnapped her, anyway? If she did in fact make it to the grocery store, this perpetrator would have had to intercept her in the parking lot, which was filled with dozens of shoppers coming and going that time of day.

It didn't make sense. The idea that she got a bug up her butt to head out into the woods for a quick hike made more sense, although even that seemed bizarre to Charlie.

"What about posting on social media? Like Facebook?"

"Huh?" Charlie wasn't sure what she was talking about at first. What did that have to do with Judy? Judy used Facebook, but he didn't know how often she was on there or what she even posted. And then he understood. "Oh! Right. Like to use it to find her. I guess that's a good idea. But I don't have a Facebook account."

"I can do that in the morning, first thing. Find some local groups where I can post a message. I'll call the local newspapers, too. Have them write a story. The more eyes we have on this situation, the better."

"Good idea," Charlie said and switched on his high beams as he turned off the highway and onto County Road 1. On the left side of the road was an old Grange building surrounded by acres of pasture with cut hay. On the other side a cluster of deer stood close to the road grazing the grass along the irrigation ditch. Charlie slowed down. "The sheriff did call a search-and-rescue team out there today. It's a large area to cover, especially because we have no idea where she ended up. They're going to continue the search in the morning."

The road curved around to the left and headed south. Charlie left the brights on to see the road better. The pavement ended, the dirt portion of the road began, and the car jerked down suddenly when the tires hit a pothole. Charlie cursed under his breath. He was distracted and forgot to swerve to avoid that one. He'd learned to memorize where the potholes developed in be-tween times when the county decided to scrape the road.

"What's the road like where she was headed?" Melissa asked.

"Similar to this. Dirt."

"So her Subaru would have been okay?"

"Yes, her car could handle a lot worse than this," he added, then swerved around another pothole. His truck hit a patch of washboard around another curve and the back tires skidded slightly across the road.

Melissa looked at the dim glow of interior lights in a few homes visible from the road. Otherwise, there was just the dark outlines of piñons and junipers beyond the glow of the truck's headlights, and the darker outline of the mountains further south and to the east. A mouse skittered across the road in front of the truck, and Melissa chuckled. She'd never seen a mouse crossing a road.

Charlie and Judy lived in a stucco and stone facade ranch home in a golf course community on the mesa. They had fallen in love with the house when the realtor showed it to them. It was a bit of a stretch for them financially, and was a source of more than a few arguments over the years. But they eventually relaxed about it. Judy had loved furnishing and decorating the house. The outdoor landscaping had been Charlie's hobby. He created curved beds and planted drought-tolerant and deer-resistant flowers and Russian sage, along with several aspen trees and blue spruce.

He pulled into the garage, and they entered through the fire door. Charlie had left the kitchen and living room lights on so they wouldn't be entering a dark house. Melissa wheeled her suitcase to the guest room.

"Would you like any tea or a sandwich or anything?" asked Charlie.

"No, I'm okay, Dad. I'm going to turn in if that's alright with you. I'm kinda wiped out from the day."

Charlie nodded. He went into the kitchen, opened the refrigerator, and inspected the contents. There wasn't much left with which to make a meal, which wasn't surprising since Judy had been on her way to get groceries and never made it back. He'd have to stop by the store tomorrow at some point—or ask Melissa to do it.

He found a single can of beer left and grabbed it from the back of the top shelf, opening it on the way out to the French door that led out to their patio. He settled into one of the heavy wicker chairs and looked up at the sky. As his eyes adjusted, he enjoyed looking at the full array of stars that were visible in this dark part of the country. He wondered if Judy was out there right now, looking at these same stars, feeling despondent that she was lost and alone.

He guessed that it was 60 degrees. Not very cold, but chilly enough to be uncomfortable sleeping out in the open. Hopefully she could take shelter in her car and be okay. Maybe she'd been hiking around and then, when she was ready to head back, her car wouldn't start and her cellphone didn't have service. That was very possible. There were so few people up on the plateau with whom to hitch a ride or ask for help. But that didn't mean there weren't *any*. There were plenty of people camping this time of year. Some mountain bikers, too. It was too early for hunting season, but Charlie guessed people went up there for other reasons this time of year. Surely, she could have walked back down Divide Road a few miles until she passed someone?

His mind went in circles with the various possibilities.

Maybe she decided to stay put and stay in her car. But she wouldn't have enough water to sustain her for many more days. That was more problematic in his mind. There were no rivers or lakes up where she went as far as he could remember, but he wasn't sure.

By the time Charlie finished his beer and went inside, the moon was rising over the crest of the Cimarron Range to the east, visible from between two ponderosas and flanking the right side of his neighbor's house across the street. It was in its sharp sliver stage, the Earth casting a shadow across most of the surface of the orb. He wondered how dark it must be on the shadowed side of the moon. Probably darker than the darkest of night skies on Earth.

*

Two other sheriff deputies arrived the next morning to ask Charlie some more questions about Judy. Some of the questions were about their relationship. Had they argued the day she disappeared? Was she often going on walks or hikes by herself? Had she been in contact with anyone on the internet, like from Craigslist or Facebook, to exchange goods? Was she acting strange or secretive in the days leading up to her disappearance?

Charlie shook his head and said that they didn't even have a conversation the day she left, and if she did any of the other things, he didn't know. He didn't think so.

The search and rescue team was covering all the known trails on the plateau close to Divide Road, where Charlie had searched. They dispatched a helicopter to search the area for her car. Charlie told the deputies that his neighbor was going to take some ATVs up later that day to do their own search.

"Have you been able to review her emails for anything suspicious?" asked the older deputy, a big man with a barrel chest and a thin, graying goatee, who'd introduced himself as Don.

"I only saw spam in her email on Friday."

"What about the days before? Or even weeks before?"

"I didn't check that far back." Charlie felt exasperated and overwhelmed. He had to start writing some of this down. His brain was foggy. He hadn't slept well.

Melissa got up from where she was working on her laptop in the living room and stood next to Charlie. "Dad, maybe we can do that later, together." She looked up at the younger deputy, a shorter man with an athletic build and dark blonde hair cut close to his scalp, who said his name was Kurt. "I just posted on a bunch of local groups on Facebook asking if anyone has seen her or her car." He nodded and then turned his head to look out the dining room window.

"Looks like your friend is already here with the ATVs," said Don.

Charlie excused himself to go down to his driveway to meet Tim and the two men who were with him in his black Dodge RAM truck. Melissa sat down in the empty chair across from the older deputy.

"In your experience, what is the most likely scenario here?" she asked them.

Don rubbed his goatee and let out a long breath. "Well, in these types of situations, it's likely that she got lost up there. People go missing while hiking all the time in southwest Colorado."

"But don't you think it's weird that she would just go hiking instead of grocery shopping?" Melissa asked.

"Sure, it's weird."

"Was your mother perhaps suffering from some sort of early dementia or Alzheimers?" Kurt asked.

"What? No. Nothing like that." Melissa crinkled her brow. "You mean like she got confused?"

"Yes."

Melissa thought about the last conversation she had with her mother on the phone. She didn't *seem* confused or out of it. Not at all. In fact, Melissa was always impressed at how sharp and intuitive her mother was. She had a great memory. She remembered all of Melissa's friends' names and would remind Melissa of things she had said even when Melissa had forgotten. She loved telling Melissa about the books she was reading and had no trouble relaying the plot or citing whatever tidbits she found intriguing in the nonfiction books she liked.

"No, nothing like that. But—" Melissa cast her gaze down and suddenly remembered something. Something about their last phone conversation. Did she mention some new medication she'd been taking, that it gave her insomnia? What was the medication? Melissa poked around in the memory of that conversation. Her mother mentioned she had tried a new recipe for chicken and would send it to her (she hadn't). She asked Melissa about how work was going, but seemed a little bored when Melissa relayed a story about a difficult colleague, so she changed the subject to the remodeling project she was undertaking at her new townhome.

How had her mother seemed? A little tired, perhaps? Yes, and that's why her mother had mentioned the insomnia.

"But?" Kurt asked.

"Nothing. Just thinking about my last phone call with her." Melissa looked outside and saw Charlie nodding as one of the three men were gesturing in the direction of the ATVs. She was glad Charlie decided not to join them. He wasn't the outdoorsy type, and spending all day riding a four-wheeler probably wouldn't do his back any favors. He looked puffy and was moving slowly, too. She'd encourage him to rest later, maybe try to nap.

"Is that the last time you spoke with her?" Don asked. "When was that?"

"Maybe a couple of weeks ago? Something like that."

He nodded and wrote down something in his notebook. Then they both stood up, thanked her, told her they'd be in touch and excused themselves.

Melissa returned to the couch where she opened her laptop up and started typing.

*

Three days later there still were no leads.

The SAR team failed to find her car or any trace of her. They searched an area of roughly 150 square miles, starting not too far from where her phone last pinged to several miles up into the National Forest. There were at least a half dozen ATV and hiker trails within that area—from ones that were well-maintained and heavily trafficked by recreationists to ones that were overgrown and seldom traveled. There were no useful responses to her social media posts. There were dozens of people that commented that they'd be praying for Judy, a few that criticized why someone would go hiking unprepared and without telling anyone, and a few of her acquaintances who were shocked to learn about the situation and offered to help in any way possible.

Barb and Kathy returned, this time to drop off casseroles and cookies and to offer to search the trails themselves. Melissa told them that the SAR team had already scoured the area. What she wanted to say was not to bother, because she couldn't see how two elderly women could do a better job than an entire team trained for searching in wilderness areas. But she kept her snark in check. The food they brought over was welcome and she knew that they were as worried and heartbroken about their friend as she was about her mother.

Melissa's brother, Jack, had driven in from California and spent the day driving all over Montrose with Charlie, looking for Judy's white Subaru, in case she had, in fact, been kidnapped or had run into trouble with a local. They drove up and down the streets in the center of town, then fanned out to the country roads, farm, and ranchland west and north of Montrose. There were quite a few white Subarus in Montrose. None of them were Judy's.

A thunderstorm developed that afternoon over the plateau. It was monsoon season, when moist air from the Gulf collided with the high mesas and mountains of Colorado and created convection, often resulting in fast-moving, soaking storms in the higher elevations. Jack and Charlie watched as the clouds billowed and darkened west of town, then watched as lightning made contact with the ground somewhere in the vicinity of where they'd been searching for Judy the last several days. There weren't any structures, just a vast expanse of dark green with a few splits in the horizon that hinted at shallow canyons with seasonal creeks.

The wind picked up ahead of the storm and blew tumbleweeds and bits of trash across the highway. Jack looked at the digital temperature gauge on the dashboard. The temperature had dropped from 88 degrees to 75 degrees in a matter of minutes since the storm had moved in. Further up, it would be colder. Once it started to rain, the temperature would likely drop further still.

"How cold do you think it'll get up there after a rain?" Jack asked.

"It could get into the upper 50s, I'd guess," Charlie answered and took a sip of the coffee they'd bought from a drive-thru shop in town, "which is bad news if Judy isn't sheltering in her car."

"Yeah, she's going to get hypothermia real quick. Do you know if she had any blankets or spare jackets in the car?"

"I doubt it." Charlie sighed. The knot in his stomach was getting worse by the day. The coffee wasn't helping, but he was also fighting an ever-deepening fatigue. Every time he let his mind go to the place of imagining Judy never coming back, never being found, or of being found dead somewhere, he felt as if he were standing at the edge of an abyss so vast and dark, he felt both dizzy and paralyzed. What would he do in the days and months if that's how all this ended? He imagined waking every morning, making breakfast in his big, empty house, and tending to the flower beds that no one would care about except him.

Would he ever feel normal after that? Or would her death color the rest of his days?

His thoughts turned to Melissa and Jack. He missed spending more time with them, but he didn't think he'd necessarily want to move back to California to be closer to them if Judy died. Besides, they had their own stuff going on and wouldn't need their dad hanging around all the time, looking to ease his loneliness and grief.

The most painful thought that hounded him since Judy left the house that day was realizing he hadn't had a meaningful, intimate conversation with her in what seemed like a long time.

Their routine had diverged in recent years, and in the last few months they seemed more like roommates than husband and wife. He wasn't sure why. Laziness? Comfort? Charlie had heard that the longer you're married, the more effort it took to keep things "fresh" in a relationship. He'd simply forgotten that, or assumed they'd have more time to work on it.

Things were good when they had goals together—like moving to Ridgway, buying the house, and fixing it up to their liking. Once they reached their goals their relationship floundered, stagnated. They began to seek out their own individual goals. They stopped wondering what they were going to do together.

Their relationship was something he pushed aside, to think about and solve some other day, when he had the time and inclination. Besides, they weren't in some crisis. It was good enough, Charlie thought. They weren't miserable, were they? No, it was good enough. Besides, they had been together so long, been through so much together, knew each other so well. There was time to figure things out and to discover new goals.

We always think we have more time. And then we run out.

*

After a day spent on the computer doing some work, checking her social media posts, and then tidying up, Melissa went on a walk to loosen some of her pent-up energy and found a trail in the piñons that led to a meadow and then up a small hill. She ascended to the top. The view from there was stunning. To the east was Storm King, the northern-most and highest point of the Cimarron Ridge. To the west, the 10,000-foot-high Horsefly Peak and then the Plateau north of that, a vast ocean of green, capped by darkening clouds and a few silvery sheets of rain that smudged the sky. So different from Riverside, where she lived in a townhome surrounded by parking lots and manicured landscaping, strip malls and highways. There were hills in Riverside, too, but they were developed with homes and cypress trees and winding roads.

She relished the fresh air and quiet when she visited her parents, and could always count on feeling refreshed and relaxed after a visit. Whenever she went on walks around the mesa, her shoulder muscles would loosen and her head would clear.

Today was different, however. She couldn't find any relief from the tension that had developed at the base of her skull ever since she arrived in town. There was a sense that she was close to unraveling the unyielding mystery of her mother's whereabouts, if she could only allow herself to stay open and still long enough, both physically and mentally.

She'd had moments like that before, where she was able to intuit what she should do through some sort of extra sensory perception. She didn't know if she was simply allowing her sub-conscious wisdom to shine through any doubt or fear, or if she was really connecting to a greater power. She knew that if she could manage to quiet her mind long enough, she could alter her consciousness to something between daydreaming and meditat-ing. Then the answers would come.

She found a cactus-free patch of ground and sat down, facing west, looking into the far distance where her mother was likely struggling to find help. She assumed her mother was struggling.

But something wasn't adding up. While Melissa believed that the most obvious answer is usually the right one, in this case, she wasn't sure they were on the right track. The most likely expla-nation was that her mother had decided on an impromptu hike and that plan had gone awry, either because her car broke down or she got hurt and couldn't hike back to where she'd parked.

So then why hadn't the search teams found her car yet?

A fluttery sensation rose up in Melissa as she watched the thunderstorm releasing its store of moisture in the distance. She tried to imagine her mother getting soaked in that rain and shivering from the cold, but she couldn't. She couldn't sense any connection to the image of her mother calling out for help while she limped from tree to tree, either.

She sat with her eyes closed, breathing in and out, focusing on the blotchy shapes that formed on the inside of her eyelids. After a while, the words in her head became a buzzing vibration, devoid of language and meaning.

Melissa opened her eyes. She was certain that if her mother was out there in the woods, she would feel it. And she didn't. She and her mother shared a strong, psychic bond because so often, one of them would be thinking of the other and the phone would ring. They'd often finish each other's sentences. Or come to the same exact conclusion about something.

Therefore, it was unimaginable to her that her mother was cold, hungry and weak from dehydration after four days in the wilderness. She didn't connect to that level of distress in her gut.

Their last conversation—on the phone, a couple of weeks earlier—was too unremarkable to be their last. She hadn't even asked her why she was on a new medication or what it was for, because she'd been too preoccupied with her work drama. She felt guilty for being annoyed that her mother didn't seem more engaged in her troubles and didn't have any advice about it. Maybe she was going through something herself and Melissa didn't even ask her about it.

So much for their psychic bond.

A year prior, she and Judy had spent a couple of weeks together in late spring on a camping trip in the southwest. They hiked the trails in three national parks in Utah and the Grand Canyon in Arizona. Melissa wasn't experienced with tent camping, but Judy was. She and Charlie had taken up backpacking after Melissa and Jack had moved out of the house after high school. They'd backpacked in the Sierras and the Rockies and had learned how to read topographic maps and pack efficiently for trips lasting a week at a time. Now, Judy came prepared with all the conveniences and creature comforts, so all Melissa had to bring was a tent and a sleeping bag. Even though Melissa dreaded sleeping outside on the ground and being without WiFi for much of the trip, it turned out that she enjoyed the sense of ruggedness. She loved looking up at the Milky Way every night and waking up to the smell of campfire and sage every morning.

She and Judy never ran out of things to talk about, and they were in sync with what they were in the mood to do every day, when they needed to rest and relax, and when they each needed time to themselves.

Her mother also impressed her with her outdoor skills. She was the one who paid attention to where to turn to rejoin a trail, the one who knew exactly how much water to pack or where to find water along the trail to put through the filter. She brought trail maps and suggested their daily itinerary.

It turned out to be one of her favorite vacations.

Judy wasn't a slouch when it came to the outdoors or hiking.

So where *was* she? Melissa closed her eyes again. Some images flashed.

A highway overpass.

A hotel room.

Her mother, driving and sipping on a drink through a straw, her hair pulled back in a tiny ponytail, her face—*determined?* Or was that defiance on her face?

Melissa opened her eyes and swayed a little bit, side to side. Her mother wasn't lost, no! She had taken off on purpose. She had disappeared *on purpose.*

That felt true to her. The other thing that felt true was that she was already very far from here—not even in Colorado. Maybe she was heading west, toward California or Oregon? Why wouldn't she have called?

Then she remembered what her father told her about the bank account and credit cards, that she hadn't used them since she had gone missing. Also, that her phone was turned off or out of range and hadn't been turned on or used since. He had put a "notify me when found" instruction on the Find My Phone app and so far, it hadn't notified him.

"Well, mom, I can't figure out what you're up to, but I really don't think you're lying in a ditch somewhere out there. If you were, I'd know it." Satisfied, she got up, brushed the dirt off her butt and started walking back to the house. Jack and her dad would probably be home soon, and she would share her theory with them. Maybe they could brainstorm where she may have gone and why. Maybe she could scour her mother's email some more, look for what may have given her mother ideas on where to go. Maybe look at her browser history for hotel inquiries. Or look through her Amazon account to see what kind of books she'd read recently.

Maybe something she'd read had given her some wacky ideas. Had she joined a cult?

She picked up the pace and an hour later, walked through the unlocked side door and into her parents' house. Jack and Charlie were standing together in the kitchen, having what looked to be a serious conversation. Jack was holding her phone.

"Melissa, where were you?" Jack put her phone down.

"Sorry, I was out for a walk. How'd it go?"

"We just got a call from the sheriff." Charlie's face dropped and he reached out to brace himself against the counter.

"They found her car." Jack brought his hand to his face and his voice became thick. "They found her car, Mel," he repeated.

"What?! Where?" Melissa's thoughts shuffled through the possible answers. California, Washington, Montana. He's going to say her car was found in the Smokey Mountains. Banff, Canada. Or Florida. Yeah, Key West, some resort on the beach. In the image she'd had of her mom, wasn't she *glowing* from having been in the sun?

"Probably about twenty miles north of where we'd been searching," Jack replied. "Off Divide Road. Way off the road. Off on some four-wheel drive service road or something."

Melissa's mind clicked in to the present and she leaned her belly against the kitchen counter. Divide Road? She was really up there? That couldn't be.

"The sheriff said some rancher found her car up there, called it in. Apparently the road she was on was so rocky, she high-centered the Subaru," Charlie added. "She just kept driving for miles on that goddamn road until she high centered the god-damn car!"

Charlie's face turned red and he struck the granite counter with his fist. "What the HELL was she thinking?"

"Listen, we've got three hours before it starts getting dark, so let's not waste it standing around trying to figure this out right now," said Jack. "We'll take my truck and head up there. Grab some flashlights, jackets, water. Mel? You got that?"

Melissa looked up at her brother with her mouth agape.

"You got that?"

"Yeah, got it." But she didn't get it. It didn't make sense. She didn't want this to make sense.

*

Jack's first thought when he saw the white Outback slanting and stuck on top of a shelf of shale rock was that there was no way she was the one that drove it up there.

He'd navigated the mile of rough road from the main dirt road, but it had been tricky. He wasn't very experienced with off-roading and he hadn't had to even put the truck into four-wheel-drive since last winter when he took his kids up to Big

Bear to go skiing. He stopped well short of where the Subaru was blocking the road and he, Charlie and Melissa got out and walked the rest of the way. The shadows were getting long in between the golden orange light. It had taken them two hours to get to the location where the service road branched off. Charlie followed the directions the deputy gave him over the phone, but he still took a couple of wrong turns. The roads switch-backed, branched off and made 90-degree turns, and the signage was very poor. Thankfully, Jack had a map app on his phone that worked off GPS, because they hadn't had cell service for at least an hour.

Two sheriff vehicles, one Ouray County and one Montrose County, were parked where the service road intersected. Three deputies had walked up the rest of the way and were standing next to the Subaru. One was taking photos of the interior of the car with his phone.

Jack approached the Ouray County deputy, who looked at him with an expression of sympathy.

"What's the story here?" Jack asked him.

"The car was unlocked. The keys are still in the ignition. We found her purse on the passenger side floor. Her credit cards are still in there and she had about $40 in cash. Her iPhone is in the purse but dead, out of juice. We searched about a quarter mile out so far. Called out. No sign of her."

Melissa stood and ducked her head under the car to inspect the damage. The left front wheel wasn't contacting the ground. "Jesus, it's impaled good. Why would she have driven on this road?"

Jack went to open the car door and the deputy stopped him.

"Let's not touch anything, because at this point this could be a crime scene."

"Really?" Jack stepped back and crossed his arms. "What makes you think a crime was committed?"

"Nothing yet. I guess we won't know until we find her. Certainly nothing in the car indicates that there had been any foul play at this point. It appears she just abandoned the car."

After a few more minutes speaking to the deputies about the plan for a new search in the morning, Jack, Charlie and Melissa got the flashlights out of the RAM and started walking, agreeing to stay within sight of one another to avoid getting disoriented. Jack also turned his map app on so they could find their way back to where they started.

There were aspen trees on either side of the narrow service road but no established trail, so they had to weave their way around fallen logs and low shrubs. It was slow going. Charlie had to walk carefully to avoid hurting his knee, and their flashlights weren't yet penetrating the shadows in the fading light of dusk.

The ground sloped downward shortly after they stepped into the woods. Charlie and Melissa followed close behind Jack, who led the way. He stopped every so often to look around and decide on a direction after checking the map on his phone.

"Dad," Melissa asked Charlie, "do you know what medication mom was taking that was giving her insomnia?"

Charlie didn't answer right away. He leaned against the bark of an old aspen to stabilize himself while stepping over an old, rotting pine log. Even so, his pant leg caught a branch and he lost his balance and almost fell. He grumbled and snapped off the branch that was tugging at him.

"I don't know what medication she was taking. How do you know she was having insomnia?" Charlie asked.

"She told me when I talked with her last. She said she was feeling pretty out of it lately because she was on some medication that gave her insomnia."

"Honestly, I don't know. She didn't tell me anything about any medication."

"Don't you think it's weird that mom didn't tell you that?" Jack asked. "I mean, there seem to be a lot of things you didn't know about her. It's like you two didn't even talk to each other."

"We talked to each other. What do you mean?" Charlie's tone was defensive. "Just because she didn't tell me—"

"For all we know, Dad," Jack's voice rose in anger, "She could have taken off with someone, someone you don't know about, and that person joy-rode her car up here, and she's—"

"Jack, this isn't—" Melissa interrupted.

"No, it is, Mel! I mean, what the hell? It's like mom and dad had been living completely separate lives these last few years. When did you hear mom tell you about anything they were doing *together*? They stopped going on vacations together. They had their own friends. They did their own thing. They even had separate bedrooms."

"Alright, that's enough." Charlie caught up with Jack and was close enough that he could reach out and touch him if he wanted. "Our personal life has nothing to do with her disappearance. I don't know what you're insinuating."

Jack changed direction and picked up his pace. He didn't think his dad had anything directly to do with his mom's disappearance, but he couldn't help but feel resentful that Charlie was so passive in all of this. Jack was the one who suggested they drive around Montrose that day. He was the one who went through a checklist of possible scenarios with him, asking him about recent credit card charges on their account, taking the initiative to go through her old phone statements in case there was a clue there. He even went through their checkbook, which his mother still used to pay certain bills.

There were questions that Charlie couldn't answer. Phone numbers he didn't recognize. Charges for doctor visits and checks made out to the hospital he couldn't explain. Why couldn't he explain them? Why didn't his mother confide in her husband more? Even in the last few years during a time when his own marriage was strained, he and Shelly found things they could still talk about and share with each other.

But his parents' relationship had changed ever since they moved to Colorado. They were so convinced they would create the perfect retirement lifestyle for themselves in the mountains. But after they settled in, Judy started to complain that she felt isolated living up on the mesa, especially in the winter, when the few friends she made left to snowbird in Arizona and Texas. He remembered her complaining that Charlie continued to be a workaholic even though he was retired, and it was hard to talk him into traveling. He preferred to be at home, doing his pro-bono legal work, reading, and tinkering with the antique clocks he collected.

When they lived in Riverside, they were both still working, and had a lot of friends with whom they'd socialize every weekend. They'd go on several vacations together every year—to Europe or South America or to visit relatives on the East Coast. Their careers were satisfying, but they still looked forward to retirement. They wanted to live closer to the mountains, where they could ski and hike and enjoy nature.

But then Charlie injured his knee and couldn't ski anymore. Jack didn't know what happened to their travel bug. Maybe they lost their sense of adventure and curiosity about exploring new places. Maybe they couldn't afford it.

Jack hated to admit that sometimes he was a little resentful of his parents for moving to Colorado. Before, he could come and visit them every weekend if he wanted, take the kids over, spend the holidays with them. It's something he enjoyed (even if his wife didn't). He counted on being able to run his business ideas past Charlie, who always made it a point to be supportive, no matter what Jack decided to do. His mother was a bit more cautious and played the devil's advocate, but would always tell him that she believed in him and knew he'd always come out ahead, no matter what.

He knew he was lucky to have a good relationship with his parents. He had envisioned them being a part of his son and daughter's life in a consistent, reliable way.

Now it took effort to maintain that level of closeness. He had to carve out at least a week for a visit, and the extra expense of flying into this small mountain town wasn't inconsequential.

And now this situation.

His mom had either gotten into some sort of trouble or had lost her marbles and decided to go on some wilderness adventure by herself at the spur of the moment without informing anyone or preparing in any way. He had no idea which of the two explanations was more feasible. Was it more likely that his mother had trusted the wrong person or that she made a rash decision that she hadn't thought through?

Perhaps the latter, Jack decided. Certainly, this fit into the category of the type of outcomes he was used to when it came to his parents. The hasty acceptance of a lowball offer on their home in Riverside because they were "worried" that they wouldn't have a better offer in time to move. The purchase of expensive golf course property here when neither one of them played golf, because they liked the quality of the house and the impressive view from the living room.

They had turned their flashlights on and had only walked another half an hour before they were forced to stop and turn around because the extreme downward slope of the hill had made it too treacherous to walk in the waning light. Charlie almost fell after tripping several times over branches and rocks, and started to complain about his knee.

Jack wanted to keep searching. He knew that if his mother was still alive, she probably couldn't hang on much longer without warm clothes, water or food. He also knew he couldn't drag his father along for an all-night search without putting him at risk for getting hurt and needing his own rescue. He felt impatient and aggravated. He took longer strides back up the slope and weighed his options. Maybe he could ask the deputies to drive them home while he stayed back and continued the search? If they were still there at the car.

"Jack! Wait up!" Melissa pleaded.

Jack turned around and watched as she took Charlie's arm to help stabilize him as he stepped over a dark obstacle Jack couldn't see.

"We're going back," Jack shouted. "Maybe you two can stay in the car while I keep searching."

Melissa mumbled something while Jack waited, sweeping his flashlight slowly in an arc into the shadows between the trees. The wind picked up and the tops of the aspens swayed above him. A few stars twinkled in the sky. The faint sound of a car engine rumbled somewhere far away.

By the time they made their way back to the Subaru the deputies were gone. Jack glanced inside the passenger window and noted that his mother's purse was gone, so he guessed they must have taken it as evidence, or were reticent to leave it in case someone else found the car. The temperature had dropped significantly since sunset, and all three of them were feeling uncomfortably chilled. They got to the truck and put on the jackets they'd left in the back seat.

Jack looked around at the inky silhouettes of the trees that loomed over them on all sides, feeling the weight of night upon him like malevolent specter. He looked at his phone to check the time. He rubbed his eyes and yawned.

"I don't think we're going to be of any help up here tonight," he concluded and opened the driver's side door of the truck.

"I think you're right. We should go home. Pick this up in the morning," Charlie added. He got in the front passenger seat and snapped in his seatbelt.

As they made their way back over the bumps and ruts to Divide Road, Melissa scooted forward in the backseat and rested her elbows on top of the center console.

"I just don't think she's here," she said, looking straight ahead at the road. "I have a feeling someone else drove her car up here, got stuck, and took off. I don't know how or why, and I can't explain it. All I know is that I feel in my heart she's not here. She's not lost. She's not dead." She put her face down in her hands and sobbed.

Jack hunched his shoulders and kept his hands on the steering wheel. Charlie reached over and put his arm around Melissa, pulling her toward him, constrained by the awkward position of their bodies in proximity to each other.

They rode in silence most of the way back.

*

The publicity generated by the local newspapers and social media that Judy's Subaru was found in such a remote part of the Plateau resulted in dozens of volunteers offering to help with the search.

They brought their ATVs, motorbikes and bicycles. They drove up and searched on foot, in small groups, bushwhacking through the woods and canyons and hillsides, extending several miles in every direction from the abandoned car, which had since been towed out of the area and taken to a mechanic.

Law enforcement deployed a helicopter to the area two days in a row but suspended that mode of reconnaissance when it failed to yield any results. The consensus was that it would be difficult to locate a body in the densely treed area, and if Judy was still alive, she may not be able to signal for help in a manner that would attract the attention of an aircraft.

Volunteers followed instructions to perform a grid search from several starting points but failed to find any evidence of Judy.

If she walked away from her car, she didn't drop anything, make a fire, or leave any kind of organic signal of her distress, such as a pile of rocks or branches in the shape of letters or symbols.

A topographic map of the area was photocopied and produced to the size of a large poster and kept inside Jack's parked RAM —the informal headquarters on Divide Road where volunteers could come and highlight the areas where they had searched with a yellow marker.

Charlie conferred with search and rescue crews and instructed volunteers on which yet-unexplored areas to cover.

Melissa brought snacks and water bottles for volunteers. She updated the status of the search on social media in the evenings after she, Jack and Charlie went back to Charlie's house to eat dinner and sleep.

They inspected Judy's purse when the sheriff returned it to Charlie. They found a couple of lip balms, a tube of moisturizer, her wallet, wadded tissues and two pairs of reading glasses and a prescription bottle of antidepressants. Melissa Googled the side effects of that particular formulation of SSRI and learned that insomnia was one of them.

Judy's friends and neighbors offered their support and volunteered to assist with the search. They also brought food to the search area or dropped off care packages at Charlie and Judy's house in the morning, with muffins, sandwiches and energy bars. Kathy and Barb put the word out to those who weren't on Facebook or hadn't read the local paper's account of Judy's disappearance.

This frenzy of activity went on for five days.

With each passing day, Melissa was more and more convinced they were wasting their time because her mother wasn't even in Colorado. If she was depressed, she may have decided to go away somewhere and get some perspective. She may have taken some cash she had saved up or was staying with a friend. But neither Jack nor Charlie took her theory seriously.

Charlie was resigned to the idea that Judy wouldn't be found alive and started to make mental plans of what he would need to handle in coming months.

Jack became increasingly agitated, torn between needing to find his mother and get closure with the situation, and needing to get back home to take care of his own family. He shared in Charlie's sentiment that Judy was likely no longer alive.

By the fifth day, there were only a handful of volunteers that came in the morning to continue the search.

On the sixth day, at the edge of a canyon, under a large juniper tree, about five miles from where the Subaru was abandoned, one of the volunteers found her body.

*

Ten days earlier

Judy didn't have a formal plan.

In fact, she was, for what seemed like the first time in a long time—maybe the first time in her entire life—simply doing what her soul was telling her to do.

Instead of driving straight through to the grocery store, she made a left turn and drove west toward the Plateau. She didn't want to stop until she felt embraced by the forest. Her entire body ached with grief and terror. She couldn't even imagine any-thing—other than the smell of the aspens and the sound of the birds—that would give her relief from the thoughts that had been hounding her for the last week.

There's no future for me.

There's only suffering.

Great, debilitating suffering. Pain. Agony.

Jack and Melissa—especially Melissa—will be heartbroken when they find out. Don't want to imagine their suffering.

There's no hope. No happiness anymore. No tomorrow that's worth it.

She didn't care anymore. She didn't care how far she had to drive. She didn't care if her car had enough gas. She no longer feared what would happen or whom she would disappoint.

She wasn't even angry at her body anymore. When she tried to sense that part of her abdomen that was growing uncontrolled and taking over, she couldn't. She couldn't feel it. It was as if it was mocking her, making her question whether she was imagining the whole thing, whether the doctors and radiologists had made a mistake.

She knew that her mind was struggling to survive, and it was desperately trying to change her mind by telling her lies.

But she was done listening to it, one way or the other. Her soul was in the driver's seat now. And after a while, it decided to turn off the main road and tuck into the aspens.

When she heard the awful scraping sound and the car would no longer move forward, she put it in park, turned off the engine and just sat, weeping, her forehead on the steering wheel, tears streaking down her cheeks.

She sat up and stared straight ahead, feeling numb and heavy. She didn't bother checking her phone. There was no reason to.

The sun was shining and the sky was so blue, so clear, so damn *optimistic*. The trees were neither friendly nor hostile, which was a disappointment to Judy. She had hoped they'd be more inviting. They weren't. She couldn't see the mountains or anything other than the damned trees. She wanted to see the mountains, at least. So she got out of the car, walked down the bumpy trail back to the main road and turned left. She wanted to walk to a clearing or a hill at least. But after a few minutes she changed her mind about walking on the road because she felt exposed. She loathed the idea of someone driving past and asking her if she needed help, even though traffic was virtually nonexistent. She'd passed only a few vehicles on the way up. Nevertheless, she stepped off the road and walked parallel to it in the woods.

The sun started to go down by the time she found a clearing and what appeared to be a slight rise in the landscape. She was out of the aspens and back in ponderosas, piñons and junipers. She set her sights on the highest point in the direction of the setting sun and walked in that direction. Her pace was slowing. She was tired and thirsty. The pain in her side was back, too. Maybe her mind had given up on trying to gaslight her into thinking everything was okay.

She finally reached what turned out to be the edge of a cliff overlooking a canyon with cottonwoods and large, red rocks and small, light green shrubs. The canyon was deep and the walls were steep, almost vertical. She spotted a crooked, large juniper close to the edge and walked slowly towards it, her breath now coming in shorter gasps as the pain in her side intensified.

The tree's branches spread out wide and sheltered her from the glare of the setting sun. She used a stick to clear off a small area close to the trunk where she lay down. The skin on the back of her upper arms felt cold even though the rest of her body was sweating. She wished she had a sweater for later, but too late for that. She curled up and looked straight to the other side of the canyon. She suspected that she was facing the wrong direction, and even if she could see any mountains, they'd be the La Sals in Utah.

As her breath finally recovered from her uphill climb, and her heartbeat slowed, the silence of the wilderness permeated her awareness. There were no mechanized sounds. Just the occasional *kruk kruk* from a crow or the *swooshhhh* sound the breeze made as it passed through the trees.

Oddly, she felt less alone here than she felt at home. There were less reminders of her aloneness. She didn't have to check her phone for unanswered text messages. Charlie wasn't in the next room, clicking away on his keyboard or having a phone conversation with someone about *something of consequence*. There wasn't a TV to remind her that she wouldn't know what would happen in the next election or whether or not humanity ever solved climate change or if the History Channel would produce another season of her favorite show.

She didn't want her Ridgway friends to feel sorry for her. And her Riverside friends had already moved on after she had moved away. She would become a cautionary tale for them, at best. *Live your life to the fullest because you never know*, they'd whisper to each other, shaking their heads while ignoring their own advice.

And Charlie? She and Charlie once had a close, companionable marriage. That was years ago. She didn't know why it went wrong or how to get back to the easy affection and effortless conversations. He started scoffing at anything she wanted to do or buy. "Too expensive. Not my thing. I wouldn't be caught dead doing that," he'd say.

She'd grown resentful.

He had become silent and mean.

"Screw him," she said out loud to the tree, then coughed to clear the phlegm out of her throat.

She stretched out on her stomach and rested her head on her forearms, inhaling the smell of the earth below her nose. Even though she had cleared most of the juniper needles and dead branches, the ground was still unbearably lumpy and therefore, very uncomfortable.

This was nothing compared to what was in store for her, she thought. What *would* be in store for her, whether she stayed here or went home.

Eventually, the fatigue from the hike and the emotional roller coaster of the previous week overwhelmed the discomfort of her soft body on the unyielding ground, the cold, the thirst, and the internal pains. She fell asleep under the tree.

At sunrise, she emerged from a long dream and floated to the surface of wakefulness. Still holding on to the images of that dream, her eyes opened to slits, taking in a new day. Her vision filled with reddish brown soil and dusty blue sky.

She closed her eyes again and remembered.

She'd been walking a long time, hiking a trail with hundreds— maybe thousands of people. The trail was winding up a mountain that was devoid of vegetation, just cliffs and spires and rocky outcroppings. Water and snow cascaded down the slope, slowing her progress. She didn't know how much farther she had to go, but she knew that once she reached the top she could rest and be safe. She couldn't turn around or stop for too long. She had to keep going until she got to the top.

A few people passed her on the trail and scolded her. They asked why she hadn't been more prepared. She replied that she didn't even know she was supposed to be here, so how could she have prepared?

Strange dream, she thought. It was one she'd had before— the mountain, the trail, the obstacles, the avalanches. Needing to reach the summit of a mountain only to get a view of the barren landscape below.

Was this her life?

She supposed it was.

It probably was.

| 41 |

RETREAT

"The soul faithfully comes to our aid through dreams,
deep emotion, love, the quiet voice of guidance, syn-
chronicities, revelations, hunches, and visions, and at
times through illness, nightmares, and terrors."
— Bill Plotkin, *Nature and the Human Soul*

The property caretaker was late.

Luca looked at the digital time display on the dash of his rental Jeep and verified that the man was, specifically, half an hour late. It was 1:30 p.m. Luca checked his phone and noted the two signal bars but no text messages or calls. He would wait five more minutes and then call him.

He was parked in front of a four-foot-tall berm of snow in a large parking area that had been plowed or shoveled recently. Several vehicles were parked nearby, all of them either SUVs, trucks, or Subarus. Some were covered in a foot of snow. On the other side of the parking area he saw snowmobiles—some covered with a tarp, some not. The road up to this point had been snowpacked and icy in spots. He hadn't passed a single vehicle since turning off the state highway.

He re-read the directions the caretaker had emailed him that he had printed out and stuck in the cubby underneath the car's stereo:

At the light, turn right. Go straight through the town of Ridgway, and the road will become highway 62. Keep going another ten miles, over the Dallas Divide. Take a left at the brown sign that says Last Dollar Road. Drive approximately six miles until the road ends at a parking lot. I'll meet you at 1.

The directions were fairly straightforward, and he didn't think he made any wrong turns getting here from the airport in Montrose. He was in the right place; he was sure of it. The guy was just late, which was aggravating. Luca managed to make it on time despite a flight delay, a snafu at the car rental counter, and a stop at the Ridgway Mountain Market for groceries and supplies. All this guy had to do was get here from wherever he lived nearby.

Luca rubbed his eyes and leaned his head back against the headrest.

The sky was overcast with a thin layer of clouds that gave the meager sunlight a sickly sheen. It was early January, so it felt like the day was quickly slipping away and sunset was imminent. He wasn't sure how long it was going to take to get to where he was going, and he dreaded the idea of arriving after dark.

He checked his phone again.

1:32.

"C'mon, c'mon!" Luca grumbled.

Despite this minor annoyance, the drive up had mesmerized Luca. The mountain range on his left rivaled anything he'd seen on his trips to Alaska and the Austrian Alps. The undulating expanse to his right was flat white with undisturbed snow, with dispersed stands of white-barked aspens. Beyond that, he saw larger snow-shrouded hills, not quite as majestic as the mountains, but beautiful in their own wildness and scope.

As relatively undeveloped this place was, it wasn't a complete wilderness. There were at least a few people residing in this remote area—he passed several timber ranch gates and several log homes with vehicles parked on the side and smoke drifting out of the chimney. Judging from the number of cars parked next to him, there must also be homes or cabins out beyond what he could see past the berm, where the land sloped downward toward a thick stand of aspen before gradually ascending into an evergreen forest.

Before he could check the time again, he heard the rumble of an engine approaching behind him. He looked in the rear-view mirror and saw a blue Ford truck—an older model with a plow attached to the front—pulling in and parking close to the snowmobiles.

Luca got out of the Jeep and walked around to see if the man in the Ford made eye contact and recognized him as the person he was meeting.

A stocky man dressed in tan Carhart overalls and a stained, plaid coat got out of the truck. He was in his 30s, had a full beard, and wore a black knit cap. He looked up at Luca and approached him without smiling.

"Hey, sorry I'm late. I had to help pull a neighbor out of a ditch. He took a turn too fast," he extended his hand and finally softened his expression. "I'm Shane. You're Luca, I'm assuming?"

Luca shook the man's bare, meaty hand with his own gloved one. "Yes, hi. Glad I'm in the right place."

"A-yup. You're in the right place. Alright, so let me get this set up and we'll get going."

Shane opened the tailgate of his pickup and pulled out a black plastic tub sled with a tow bar in the front. He pulled it over to one of the snowmobiles that were covered in a tarp and a few inches of snow and attached it to the back. Then he removed the tarp and folded it up, placing it in the bed of his truck.

"You've got stuff you're bringing to the cabin, yeah?" He asked Luca. "Go ahead and put it in the sled."

Luca pulled several full grocery bags and a duffel out of the backseat of the Jeep and walked over to the sled, where he loaded everything. He noticed an elastic hemmed cargo cover, so he secured it over the bags—like a shower cap.

Meanwhile, Shane started the ignition of the snowmobile, which caught after a few tries and spewed sooty exhaust in Luca's direction. He revved the engine a few times and then let it idle. He hopped off and got on another snowmobile and repeated the process.

Luca made sure he had the keys to the Jeep in the front pocket of his parka and zipped it shut. He pulled his hat down further over his ears and stepped toward the snowmobile.

"You ever ride one?" asked Shane, walking back to the first snowmobile while pointing to it.

"No."

"It's simple; I'll show ya."

Shane waited for Luca to get on the seat.

"Here's where you start it or cut the engine. Here's the choke. Pull it up before you pull the cord here. To accelerate, press this in. To stop, just release. If you need to stop faster, press the left trigger here," Shane pointed to the brake on the left handlebar. Luca nodded, placing his hands on the handlebars and squeezing the accelerator. The machine purred.

Shane walked back over to his truck. He got two helmets out and handed one to Luca, who put it on and snapped the strap under his chin.

"Alright, follow me, but not too close. You don't want to slide into me if I stop abruptly. And punch it on the last uphill. It's steep, so if you don't go fast enough, you'll stall."

Luca gave Shane a thumbs up and released the brake, then gingerly squeezed the accelerator again, and the machine lurched forward. He felt a tingle of excitement as his snowmobile powered through a short ledge of snow and ice and glided effortlessly forward. He sped up to keep up with Shane, who blazed up an incline, following along established tracks toward the trees.

Luca's cheeks and neck got blasted with the icy sting of cold air. He rebuked himself for not putting on the gaiter he packed. Despite the initial discomfort, Luca inhaled the fresh mountain air and exhaled through his pursed lips, allowing his gut to release the tension he'd been holding since he rushed out the door on the way to the airport that morning.

He had made the right decision coming here. The views were spectacular. It was quiet and remote. He was looking forward to arriving at the cabin he rented, making a cup of hot tea, and relaxing in front of the fireplace later without worrying about phone calls, emails, Zoom meetings, or bullshit documentation waiting for his review.

He noticed that Shane had veered off the main set of established snowmobile tracks, which looked like they followed a road, and had started climbing up the side of the hill into the woods. He lost sight of him for a few minutes but followed his tracks through the woods, up and down over bumps and valleys, and around boulders and fallen trees. The slope was gradual, and the ride was pleasant. Occasionally he would catch a glimpse of a distant mountain range to the west. But his gaze couldn't linger long. He had to stay focused to keep from hitting trees or veering off track.

After going up and over the hill, they entered a clearing and rejoined the main road below. He wondered if Shane had just taken a shortcut or if he was joyriding for the heck of it. The road straightened out, Shane sped up and Luca followed suit. Luca wondered who these snowmobiles belonged to. Shane? The owner of the cabin? Someone else? One more thing to ask Shane once they got to the destination.

The road curved left and the ground to the right sloped sharply, exposing a narrow ledge about the width of two cars. Luca's stomach lurched, his body stiffening with the idea of keeping as far away from the edge as he could while still maintaining control of the snowmobile. They snaked up the road, around three switch-backs, before dipping down on the other side and back into the aspens and evergreens. The mountain range in the distance was fully visible now, the conical peaks gleaming white, towering over the skirt of rock and forest, spilling out over the snow-covered valley below them. The sky was the same color as the snow in places, creating the illusion that the mountains were merging with the clouds.

Ten minutes later, they passed a large, log house that was set back a short distance from the road and behind a metal gate. Shane stopped his snowmobile in front of the gate, got out, and swung the gate open. He waited for Luca to pass through, then hopped back on his snowmobile and passed him to take the lead up. The snow here was powdery and looked like it hadn't been disturbed recently, but there were some softly blanketed ruts indicating that someone had ridden up here before the last storm. They rode past the house, which Luca assumed was the cabin owner's main residence, and up a narrow, wooded trail. Almost immediately the slope increased, and Luca felt the snow-mobile slow down and lose traction slightly in the deep snow. He remembered to give the machine more power and was soon following right behind Shane, who expertly maneuvered up the hill, his backside off the seat and torso leaning forward over the handlebars.

How far up is this place? Luca wondered, and then remem-bered Shane mentioning something about the "last half mile". He looked back to make sure the sled was still attached, and contin-ued to push up the hill, his face completely numb and his fingers painfully throbbing from the vibration and cold.

This was as remote as Luca imagined. In the photos he saw on-line, the cabin was perched at the top of a small, wooded ravine. The photos were taken in the summer, when the sky was blue and the sun gave the place a friendly, welcoming, accessible vibe.

He hadn't checked the location on a map and there weren't any photos of the place in winter. The listing read:

Guest log cabin on a 200-acre ranch, fully equipped, with 1 bedroom and 1 bath, overlooking Mt. Wilson and Wilson Peak. Only a 20-minute drive to Telluride via a 4-wheel-drive road. Perfect romantic getaway for couples. Fully equipped kitchen, comfortable queen bed, bathroom, wood-burning stove, and a covered porch perfect for watching the sunset.

He had learned about this cabin from a colleague who had rented it for a week the previous summer. Luca looked it up on AirBNB and determined it was perfect for what he had in mind, which was an out-of-the-way place somewhere in the mountains that was quiet and secluded, but not completely rustic.

The only problem was that when he'd had this idea, it was late December, and he didn't want to wait until summer. He contacted the owner and offered to pay extra to have the place de-winterized and then re-winterized after his stay, and was glad he agreed. He was worried that if he waited, he'd find a reason not to go. There were always deals that he was in the middle of at work, always deadlines that couldn't be pushed back, always urgent situations he had to handle. Two weeks was a long time for him to be out of commission, especially when he knew he'd be completely incommunicado, since the owner warned him: no cell service, no internet, no phone. Not even a television or a radio, for that matter.

Luca's wife, Laura, told him she thought his idea was a bit over-the-top, and that she was worried that he wouldn't have any way of calling out if he needed help. Luca conceded that she had a point. Normally, this lack of communication with the outside world would be an instant disqualifier in Luca's mind when choosing a vacation rental, but this time, it was exactly what he was looking for. He didn't want a place where he would be tempted to check emails and watch the news. This time, it was critical that he be without those distractions, those intrusions, those stressors.

Laura had accepted his reasoning with pursed lips and an exasperated sigh.

Luca's 16-year-old son, Jordan, told Luca the location sounded "sick" (which was a youthful colloquialism for "awesome") and had expressed a half-hearted desire to come along. When Luca emphasized the lack of WIFI, Jordan responded with an, "Oh, never mind, then." Luca was glad Jordan retracted his enthusiasm for joining him without Luca needing to go into a lengthy and unnecessary explanation.

The driveway gradually leveled out, they crested the hill, and Luca got his first glimpse of the single-story, dark-stained log cabin he recognized from the photos. The roof was covered in a billowy blanket of snow and a few short icicles hung from the edge. There was a chimney, but no smoke. The main entrance appeared to be on the side, with a portico over the door. There was a ten-foot-wide and six-foot-high pile of firewood stacked next to the door on the side of the cabin, partially covered with a green tarp. On the narrow porch were two red Adirondack chairs with a small metal table in the middle and a door that led into the house.

It was a bewitching refuge from the harsh winter landscape.

Luca parked the snowmobile next to Shane's, who had already gotten off and was opening the side door. He disappeared inside for a few minutes, then came back out.

"Shit, I should have come up here sooner to get the woodstove going. Sorry about that." He moved to help Luca unload the supplies and bring them inside the cabin.

Luca's shoulders sank with disappointment that he wouldn't be entering a warm space. He followed Shane inside and dropped his duffel on the floor next to the couch.

"I can handle getting a fire going. Don't worry about it," he said.

The cabin was much more spacious on the inside than it looked from the outside, but still a bit smaller than it appeared in the photos. There was a woodstove facing a recliner and a couch in the middle of the living room, a modest kitchen with a narrow, chrome refrigerator, a gas stove, and a stainless-steel sink. In between the kitchen and the couch was a wooden, painted table with two chairs. There was a bedroom visible off the living room behind a colorful curtain serving as a privacy screen, instead of a door.

"You sure? I can bring some firewood in for you, how about that?" Shane asked.

"Yeah, whatever, it's fine." Even though they just arrived minutes ago, Luca wanted this guy to leave already.

Shane hauled in several armfuls of split wood and placed it next to the woodstove while Luca looked in the kitchen cabinets to take stock of what was there. A few glasses, mugs, plates, silverware, a couple of cast iron skillets, and a quart-sized metal soup pot. There was a metal press pot for coffee and a tea kettle on the gas stove. Shane turned the faucet on in the sink. Nothing came out.

"Oh, hang on, I have to switch on the pumps," said Shane. He disappeared into a closet-sized room off the kitchen and flipped a switch on the outlet panel next to the main entrance. The muffled sound of a motor emanated from somewhere under the floorboards. Shane smiled at Luca. "Well water. Pumped up to a tank in that utility closet there, and also the water heater. Then boosted by another pump to give you pressure. Solar powered pumps. Give it a minute and you'll have water. You'll need to flush out the antifreeze in the toilet, though, before using it."

"This place is solar-powered?" Luca hadn't noticed solar panels on the roof, which were covered in snow.

"Yeah, solar powered lights and pump, propane range, water heater, and refrigerator.

The heat is all from the woodstove. Unfortunately. Since this place isn't usually rented in winter. But there's plenty of firewood, so you should be good for the time you're here."

"Where are the panels?" Luca was thinking that he may need to brush the snow off to keep them functional.

"They're on the other side of the house, ground-mounted. Which reminds me, I have to check to make sure they don't have snow on them. Should be ok, though, it was sunny yesterday. Melts the snow right off at this altitude."

Luca opened the refrigerator and noted that no light illuminated the interior. He stuck his hand into the cavity but couldn't tell if it was working or not, since the temperature in the house was also close to freezing. He thought that if worse came to worst, he could put the food items in need of refrigeration outside in the snow. That would certainly add to the rustic vibe of this adventure.

"This on?" he asked Shane, pointing to the unit.

"Should be."

Luca turned his back to Shane, facing the bags of groceries, and mumbled to himself in a hushed tone so Shane wouldn't hear. "*Should be. Awesome.*"

Shane stood silently and watched as Luca took groceries out of bags and placed them on the shelves inside the refrigerator. Vanilla almond milk, a six-pack of beer, a gallon of spring water, a quart of non-dairy creamer, a tub of margarine, a loaf of whole-grain bread, jam, three packages of turkey hot dogs, and a jar of peanut butter.

"I gotta say, I was expecting a couple. Is your wife or girlfriend joining you later?" Shane asked.

"No. I'm here alone." Luca replied, his expression sanguine. *Funny that the guy assumes I have a wife or girlfriend. This sure isn't the Bay area.*

In response, Shane raised his eyebrows, wanting to ask, but hesitating.

"No one is joining me later," Luca added, "I came here to get away."

"I see," Shane nodded, his voice barely louder than a whisper. "It can get pretty quiet up here, though, especially this time of year. If you're not used to the solitude. Or the dark."

Luca scoffed. "The *dark*, really? I'm not afraid of the dark."

"It can creep people out," Shane shrugged. "Just sayin'."

"I can handle it," Luca responded, his tone slightly abrasive.

Jesus, does this guy think I'm some city slicker wuss? Luca asked himself. *I've spent Decembers working in Stockholm. I've been to Alaska in the middle of winter when the sun doesn't even come up for more than 3-1/2 hours a day. Dude, this is Colorado in January. Get a grip.*

He stacked the cans and jars of organic chili, soup, and spaghetti sauce on the counter and put bags of pasta and rice next to them. Then he placed a box of high-fiber cereal, a couple boxes of tea, a container of oatmeal, and a bag of ground coffee in one of the cupboards that had space for it. He scrunched up the plastic bags and looked around the kitchen for a place to put them, found the trash basket under the sink, and threw them away.

"Ok, that's cool." Shane said, "But if you need something, you know you don't have cell service up here. You can take the snowmobile back to your car, where you'll be able to text me. You *shouldn't* run into any issues, but just in case, that's probably the first place you'll have a signal because it's around the mountain. You can go the other way toward Telluride, but I wouldn't recommend it. Too far to go for a signal. There's a notebook on the coffee table with some instructions about the appliances and stuff. There are some snowshoes and poles on the porch if you want to go exploring, too."

"Great, thanks," said Luca and put his hands in his front pant pockets. "Is there enough gas in the snowmobile?"

"Like for riding around or something?"

"No, for getting back."

"It's got a full tank. You'll be fine for getting back," said Shane.

Luca noticed that Shane's nose was glistening with snot and his cheeks were ruddy from the cold. His hands were buried in his overalls. Had he ridden all this way without gloves?

No matter, it was none of his business. Luca didn't live around here but at least he came prepared with gloves and oh, by the way, *he wasn't afraid of the dark, either.*

Shane took a step backward toward the door. "I'll be back on the 20th for the cleaning and to shut everything back up and re-winterize. But you don't need to wait for me. I'll likely show up after noon that day. If you don't mind, put an extra log or two in the woodstove before you leave."

"Roger that."

*

Luca heard Shane start his snowmobile and buzz down the hill, the sound of his departure fading quickly. As he squatted down in front of the woodstove to start the fire, a veil of silence engulfed the house. Not even the eternal low hum of a refrigerator or the drip-drip-drip of a leaky faucet.

Nothing. Just silence.

The kind of silence in which you can hear your ears hum and your heart beat. Luca closed his eyes for a few seconds and relished it. He couldn't even remember a time when he experienced this level of silence.

He looked at the pile of firewood Shane stacked and noted that it was all quarter-cut logs. No twigs or smaller pieces. He looked around the stove and found a box of long matches lying on the tile. He opened the box. Plenty of matches. Good. But he had to find some kindling.

He stepped outside and first looked around the woodpile, but didn't see any smaller piles of twigs or sticks. He would have to get into the trees. He made a mental note to clear the path from the house with the snow shovel that was leaning against the cabin next to the woodpile later. As he ventured farther out behind the cabin, he was post-holing up to his knees in the drifts.

Once he reached the trees, he ducked under the boughs and started snapping off the skinnier dead twigs and branches lower down the tree trunks. He'd gathered a good armload and carefully made his way back to the cabin. He was glad he had decided to put on his water-resistant pants instead of jeans this morning, otherwise his legs would be wet as well as cold as soon as he warmed up. Instead, the snow just sloughed off when he stomped his boots outside the door.

Back at the woodstove Luca took off his gloves and made a small triangular stack with the twigs. He placed a lit match into the center of the nest and waited for it to light. The twigs appeared to take the flame, but as soon as the match burned down, the flame extinguished. He repeated the process three times and still couldn't get the stack to light.

"Shit. Shit. Shit." Luca exclaimed, then thought for a minute. He had to get this fire going or his retreat would be over before it even started.

He stood up and looked around the living room. He noticed that one of the end tables next to the couch also served as a mini bookshelf. He walked to it and took out one of the weathered paperback books that were stacked there. It was a military thriller by Tom Clancy, at least thirty years old by the look of it. Luca returned to the stove and started tearing out the pages and crumpling them into tight wads. He placed a few under the twigs and lit another match.

As the paper caught the flame, he fed more balls of torn paperback into the fire. The twigs turned orange and a weak, but eventually steady, blue flame reached upward through the stack. Unsure his efforts would be successful, he looked around again.

There was the worn leather couch with a big quilt draped over the back. The dark green corduroy lounge chair with a flat red pillow placed in the corner of the seat. The door that led to a pantry or the water heater closet. A window with a slate-colored curtain tied back with a black, braided rope. The wooden table and two painted side chairs topped with ugly plaid cushions. The dark blue faux-marbled laminate of the kitchen counter. The food he had placed there.

The cereal box.

That could work. Also the paperboard from the six pack in the fridge, he remembered.

He got up and retrieved the boxes, removed the waxed paper bag inside the cereal box and the bottles from the six pack, and tore the paperboards into chunks that he carefully placed into the delicate flame. As the fire got more robust, he fed it more sticks until he felt confident about placing a log into the heat. He waited and watched, willing it to *please catch, please.*

Luca rubbed his bare hands together near the heat and exhaled in relief as he saw the log was taking to the flame. He then carefully placed a second log on top of the first and gently closed the stove door but didn't latch it, allowing the air to travel easily from the room up through the chimney. He monitored the fire through the glass pane.

He'd have to keep this fire going nonstop or repeat this ridiculous process each time. And there weren't enough books or cereal boxes.

What about overnight? He wasn't sure. Maybe he'd need to get up to feed it logs a few times a night. Luca didn't like that idea, but he wasn't going to worry about that now. He made a mental note to reimburse the owner for the burned book with an Amazon gift card, maybe recommend something more contemporary than Tom Clancy. Perhaps he'd send the owner *The Last Man* by Mary Shelly, a book about the last man alive after a global apocalypse that his wife Laura had recently read. Luca chuckled. How appropriate that she had finished that book right before Luca announced he was going to go on a solo retreat in a remote cabin in the mountains of Colorado.

He'd brought a couple of his own books in case he wanted to read. One, a nonfiction biography about a famous businessman and the other, a thriller about a man who is accused of a crime he didn't commit and goes on the run. Laura gave him both for Christmas, which was more of a message than a gift. The message was, *are you ever going to slow down enough to enjoy a good read?*

When they first met, Luca devoured books. One of his favorite pastimes on weekends, besides reading and sailing on San Francisco Bay, was browsing the bookstore for a new literary adventure. But in the last ten years, as Luca had gotten promotion after promotion in his job at GeoX, he'd stopped reading for pleasure. He sold his sailboat because he didn't have time to take it out enough to justify the slip fees. Now his weekends consisted of pre-dawn jogs, ending with late nights reading through contracts. In between, there was maybe dinner with Laura, a few household chores, and once in a while he'd attend one of his teenaged son's varsity football games.

That's when he was home and not out of town, traveling for work, which was one to two weeks out of a month.

Even when he did have a spare hour or two, Luca could barely sit still long enough to concentrate on plots and keep track of characters. His mind would wander to the deals he was working on for work. Ironically, he had no issue sitting for long hours—as long as he was at the office or at home working.

Recently, he began suffering from lower back stiffness, head-aches, and eyestrain.

Thank you, Laura my dear, point taken. He'd grabbed the books off his nightstand and thrown them in his duffel, in case his mind needed a diversion from his own thoughts, which at times felt annoyingly persistent. Obsessive, even.

His latest obsessive thought was that he was going to die of a heart attack.

He had a valid reason. Three months ago he started having shortness of breath on his runs and couldn't get his speed and stamina back up to his usual levels. A visit to the doctor led to a stress test and blood work and the result: His heart was still okay —for now. But he was strongly advised to change his diet and work on bringing down his stress levels, which was the likely ex-planation for his "panic attacks" while jogging. He now had a pre-scription for a statin (which he'd been taking) and one for anxiety (which he decided he didn't want to take). The doctor also recom-mended losing some weight and taking up yoga and meditation to reduce stress. But Luca wasn't about to start doing downward facing dogs and meditation was, well, Luca just couldn't seem to quiet his mind long enough to meditate for more than a minute. He felt antsy, or he'd remember something he absolutely had to take care of *immediately*. Meditating for him felt like a waste of time, neither therapeutic nor relaxing.

That's when he knew he had a problem.

If he didn't learn to shut off his brain and relax, he suspected he might not make it past middle age. His own father was 50 when he collapsed with a massive coronary, leaving behind a wife who'd never worked, a big mortgage, and a mountain of debt. What a disaster. All those years working so hard, and for what? To drop dead before he even had a chance to enjoy retirement.

Fortunately, Luca and his brother Frank were able to help their mother sell her house and downsize so she could pay off the debt and live modestly off her wages as a grocery clerk. His father had owned a plumbing business in Newark, New Jersey. He'd smoked up until his heart attack and had a habit of raging against everyone: his "lazy" employees, "moron" customers, "clueless" politicians, and especially his "good-for-nothing" sons.

Luca didn't want to end up like his father—alienated from his sons, despised by his employees, and feared by his wife. He had no close friends, and his neighbors avoided him. He was a workaholic whose idea of relaxation was getting drunk while watching sports and yelling at the TV.

Until that day when he sat in his doctor's office listening to his diagnosis, Luca thought he had created a life completely different from his father's. He was successful and admired by his colleagues. He had an impressive financial portfolio. He had a loving wife whom he adored and cherished. He had a decent relationship with his son—although he hadn't spent a lot of time with him lately. He didn't smoke and rarely drank more than a beer or two. He exercised—although not every day. He had friends—although mostly at work.

Still. By all accounts, he was nothing like his father.

And yet, he was following in his father's footsteps and about to drop dead by age 51 if he didn't get his shit together when it came to his health. He knew time was running out to turn things around.

The flames engulfed the logs and Luca could feel the warmth radiating out from the woodstove. He felt goosebumps blossom on his arms. He opened the door and added another piece of wood, poking it deeper into the cavity of the stove with the iron poker he'd removed from an adjacent stand of fireplace tools.

His stomach growled. He hadn't eaten since he grabbed an energy bar and a large coffee at the airport that morning. Now that the fire was churning well and not in danger of fizzling out, he could go into the kitchen and make himself something to eat.

He took out a soup pot, filled it with water from the faucet (from which water flowed, thankfully), and lit the stove using a Bic lighter he found in one of the drawers. Then he took out the package of turkey hot dogs and began cutting them into chunks while he waited for the water to boil. He opened a jar of sauce and took out a smaller pot into which he poured the contents and set it on the adjacent burner, then scraped the mound of turkey hot dog chunks into the sauce.

While he waited for everything to cook, he walked into the bedroom. He flipped the light switch on the wall, and one of the lamps on the aspen log nightstands illuminated. There was a queen-sized log bed with a thick comforter and an oil painting of a field of flowers hanging above the bed. To the right of the bed was a bathroom with a sink, toilet, and tiny shower stall. Luca hoped the heat from the woodstove would reach well into the bedroom and bath, or else he'd be taking some unpleasantly chilly showers and wearing his clothes to bed.

The view out the bedroom window revealed a drabber and cloudier sky since his snowmobile ride to the cabin. He guessed it was probably close to 3pm by now. The sun was starting its final descent. He had at most an hour and a half before it got too dark to explore around outside.

He ate quickly without taking off his jacket or boots since it was still frigid. But by the time he washed his dishes and pots and put them out on a towel to dry, the house had warmed up considerably, and he started to sweat a bit. He shoved more wood into the woodstove and went outside.

His plan was to get more kindling after he explored the perimeter of the property. He found the snowshoes Shane had told him about on the porch and put them on, then duck-walked off the porch and around the back of the cabin. There he saw the propane tank and the ground-mounted solar panels. There was also a small wooden shed, which he approached. He unlatched the door and looked inside. It was a tool shed of sorts: shovels, rakes, extension cords, an oil-and-sawdust-coated chainsaw, a handsaw, a hatchet, an ax, and a couple of empty orange buckets. He grabbed a bucket and a handsaw and made his way up the hill toward the trees. With the handsaw, he was able to collect twice the kindling in half the time.

He saw some sort of animal tracks in the snow coming out of the woods and curving around to follow the line of trees toward the driveway. He guessed they were deer or elk. He also saw a few lines of what appeared to be zig zagging rabbit or squirrel tracks, barely punching through the top layer of snow. He followed those tracks for a while before deciding there was nothing worth seeing under the thick canopy of forest. He turned around and walked towards where he'd parked the snowmobile. He put down the bucket and instead of following the driveway, he continued following the clearing on the south side of the cabin where it led to a wide, rocky ledge where he could stand and look down at the treetops and see further down the valley. He saw a few houses dotting the white expanse, perhaps a mile or two away. They didn't appear occupied since there was no smoke rising from their chimneys and no vehicles parked nearby. But that in itself didn't mean anything because the only access was by snowmobile, and they could have other modes of heating.

Before heading back to the warmth of the cabin, he walked halfway down the hill to stretch his legs and get some exercise. On the way back up, he was surprised at how out of shape he felt. He felt his heart pounding in his ears and his breath came in shallow gulps. He had to stop several times to catch his breath and his pace was sluggish. He felt queasy and there was a heaviness in his midsection. He feared that his heart condition had gotten worse, until he remembered that he was at high altitude—perhaps 9,000 feet or higher. That was probably the reason why he couldn't catch his breath.

When he returned to the cabin, he was glad that the fire had heated the space enough to feel comfortable. He fed a few more logs into the fire—as many as would fit—and then sat down on the couch to watch the flames engulf them.

His head and shoulders felt heavy. He'd been up since 4 a.m. and he hadn't slept well the previous night, which was not unusual for Luca. He'd often have trouble getting to sleep, then wake two to three hours later, process a work dilemma, and toss and turn for another two hours before finally slipping into an exhausted slumber a short while before the alarm clock on his phone buzzed.

He reclined on the cold leather and draped himself up to the neck with the musty smelling quilt. Gazing at the fire, his heart still hammering from the exertion of the snowshoe, his breath steady, he felt his body sink into the cushions as he slipped into unconsciousness.

*

"WHAT DO YOU THINK YOU'RE DOING?"

Luca was startled awake by a voice. He threw the quilt off himself and sat up, grabbing the back of the couch to steady himself. Did he just hear that or did he dream it? He felt disoriented, momentarily confused about where he was.

He looked around the cabin, lit by the one lamp he'd turned on. Darkness extended out beyond the reach of the light. The bedroom was a black cave and the kitchen shrouded in inky shadow. He got up and turned on the ceiling lights in the kitchen. A wave of nausea overtook him for a moment and he went to the refrigerator to pour himself some of the spring water he'd brought. Had he remembered to bring some ibuprofen? God, he hoped so. His head was pounding.

He thought he must have dreamed the voice, but it sounded so real in his head—stark and booming. A man's voice, but whose? The mental fog of his nap was slowly lifting. He found his phone and looked at the time. 6:36.

Did he smell gas? Yes, there was a subtle gas smell. Or was it the smell of the glass from which he was drinking? He stuck his nose inside it and inhaled. No, the smell wasn't from the glass. It was in the air.

He went to the utility closet and looked inside. A small water heater and tank filled with what he assumed was pumped well water, pipes that connected both, a broom, and a dustpan. He sniffed the air inside. He couldn't be sure, but he didn't think he smelled gas in there.

He then went to the refrigerator and looked behind it, seeing where a small pipe led out through the appliance and along the wall back toward the utility closet. The smell wasn't particularly strong anymore.

He walked through the bedroom and bathroom and didn't smell anything other than the subtle fragrance of whatever detergent was used on the bed linens and bathroom towels. Back in the living room the gas smell was present, but much less than before.

Great.

What would he do if there was a gas leak? There wasn't much he could do, except open the windows and air it out. But then it'd be freezing in the cabin. He imagined falling asleep and the place filling with propane, exploding into a fireball as soon as the concentration reached a critical level, igniting the woodstove or water heater pilot light.

Could he turn off the propane at the source? He pondered going out behind the cabin to examine the propane tank. For that task, he'd need a flashlight.

In the kitchen he looked in all the drawers again. Silverware, random cooking utensils, kitchen towels, some aluminum foil, a wrench and a screwdriver. No flashlight. Not even a candle. So much for that idea. How could the owner not have provided a flashlight?

He sniffed the air again. He couldn't tell if the gas had dissipated or if he'd gotten used to the smell. Hoping for the former, he refilled his water glass and sat down on the couch again. His headache was getting worse. Wasn't one symptom of propane poisoning a bad headache? It was. So was altitude sickness.

He wasn't sure what the effects of breathing in propane were.

Since the house wasn't heated by a furnace, he doubted he was getting propane poisoning. The woodstove door was latched firmly shut, and—by the look of the flames and smoke—the fire was ventilated well. He closed his eyes and relaxed his shoulders, willing the pain that radiated from the top of his head down to the back of his neck to diffuse out. He inhaled slow, deep breaths, and counted to five while exhaling.

He thought about the voice again. *What do you think you're doing?* It had asked.

Weird.

What *did* he think he was doing? Good question.

He'd rented a remote cabin in the mountains of Colorado for two weeks in order to force himself to relax. In order to *learn* to relax. To have a space of time with no distractions from work. To be able to just sit and *be present* without feeling as if he was crawling out of his skin. To learn how to meditate and de-stress so he could slip into that state more easily at home. To think about where his career was headed. To figure out what to do with the next ten or twenty years of his life.

To hopefully have an epiphany.

Tonight, however, instead of relaxing, his mind was racing with worst-case scenarios. He was not starting this project off on the right foot.

He tried to reassure himself. What were the chances that out of all the people who had rented this cabin in the previous winters, HE would be the one who would perish from the gas leak? Did the leak start right before his arrival and get worse because he used hot water to wash his dishes? Maybe the leak was always there in the background, and it was minor, nothing to worry about.

He hoped so. He wasn't even sure he'd smelled anything at all. Maybe he'd imagined it, the way he imagined the voice that woke him up.

Things will be clearer in the morning, he thought. He'd go outside and check the propane tank, maybe go for a longer snowshoe. He'd make a good breakfast for himself. Maybe journal a little bit. Read the books he brought. Do some more meditating.

He just had to get through the night first. A night that stretched out in front of him like a torturous, numbing void.

*

The gas smell didn't return, which was a relief to Luca.

It snowed on and off the next three days, adding a foot of accumulation to what was already on the ground. The evergreens were voluptuous and beautiful with fat pillows of snow weighing down the boughs. Luca spent the mornings outside, exploring the property on the snowshoes and slowly acclimating to the altitude. It was slow-going. He still got out of breath on the way back up the hill and his heartbeat thumped alarmingly loud in his ears.

He went down to the main house and snooped around, looking through the windows and admiring the timber-frame construction and contemporary mountain furnishings. He sat on the deck on the heavy wooden patio chairs and listened to the occasional crows and jays vocalizing high up in the trees. He wondered what the place was like in summer and fall, with the aspens in their full green or golden glory surrounding the house, the sun warming the deck, the smell of juicy rib-eyes cooking on the outdoor built-in grill.

Those first few mornings, he stayed outside as long as he could tolerate the cold, shoveling the snow off the driveway and wandering down in the direction of Telluride a short distance. He heard the sound of distant motors that day but didn't see any new tracks or encounter anyone out riding.

He prolonged his explorations because it gave him something to do. If he could spend four or five hours gathering sticks, clearing snow, or walking around, it was satisfying. He felt spent when he got back to the cabin and was able to take a nap without feeling guilty. He could prepare lunch and a light dinner, take his time cleaning up, do a little reading.

Once he ran out of tasks, his mood sank, and he felt a low level of dread.

The hours approaching dusk were the worst. He felt an almost unbearable restlessness. It was physical in nature. His body buzzed with an urgent energy. He needed to accomplish something, anything. One afternoon he found some cleaning products and rags under the sink and started to wipe the dust and spiderwebs from corners and crevices. With the screwdriver he found in the kitchen drawer, he tightened all the pull knobs on the cabinets. In the evenings he started reading one of the books he'd brought, but found himself re-reading paragraphs more than once. He liked the writing and found the story of the novel compelling, but it just didn't hook him. He even looked through the yellowed, old paperbacks in the side table bookcase to see if there was something there that would spark his interest more. There wasn't.

He didn't watch that much TV when he was at home. Now he wished he had TV so he could hear something other than his own breathing.

This must be what withdrawal from drugs feels like, Luca thought. *Or solitary confinement.*

Well, maybe not quite *that*. He wasn't imprisoned. He could go outside. He could even take the snowmobile out and ride around if he wanted to, get back to his car, go into town to Ridgway or Telluride. Go out to eat in a restaurant instead of eating the canned soups and stews he'd brought.

But he resisted the temptation to do that because that wasn't why he'd come here.

If he did go to town, he knew that the first thing he'd do would be to check his email. Then he'd start to make calls, arrange virtual meetings, check stats, and request data. He wouldn't come back to the cabin. There'd be too much to do. He'd book the next flight back to San Francisco and that would be the end of the retreat.

He committed himself to meditating in the afternoon and evening, but managed only about 20 minutes each time. He couldn't quell his racing thoughts, which followed a familiar theme: a regurgitation of his day or wondering how things were going at work or at home.

Puttering around a remote cabin, an idea he embraced wholeheartedly not that long ago, now seemed completely ludicrous. He pictured his colleagues at work judging him for taking two weeks off at the start of the year, which was a critical time for contracts and negotiations with mining contractors. He started to wonder if he was past his prime and could no longer hack the demands of his job. The Board was probably having that discussion now, about how he'd lost his edge and they'd need to look at replacing him.

What about Laura? Did she miss him? He surprised himself at how much he missed her. He longed for her in a way that he hadn't in years.

If he had cellphone service right now, he'd be calling her and letting her know that he loved her and regretted not being home with her and Jordan more than he had been. He hoped it wasn't too late and that his absence now wasn't pushing her to conclude their marriage wasn't working. Was he being hyperbolic? He didn't know. He'd hear stories at work about colleagues who'd been blindsided when their wives suddenly announced they wanted to separate or fell in love with someone else. The regret was almost always the same: they dropped the ball at home.

In fact, Luca wondered if Laura was acting a little distant lately. She didn't seem to care that he was doing this solo retreat, in terms of being concerned about his safety or wellbeing, or that it was so unlike him.

Was he missing something?

Stupid as usual, Luca.

That voice in his head again. But this time he wasn't asleep and he wasn't dreaming.

It wasn't his usual talk-to-himself voice, though. That's what screwed with Luca's head. The voice was faint, as if someone was saying it behind a closed door. He hadn't *consciously* composed the thought.

No matter, Luca thought. *Maybe that internal voice is right. Maybe I have been stupid. I fucked up. I've neglected my family, and now I am going to pay the price.*

Why did I do this? Why am I wasting time passing the hours in this place? Why am I so self-absorbed?

I should have taken Laura and Jordan on a two-week vacation to Hawaii instead. I could have left my phone and laptop at home. The result would have been the same, wouldn't it? Except my marriage and family would be intact.

For the first time since he'd had this idea, he doubted its merit and felt ashamed of himself. Why did he think he needed to go to such an extreme by coming here? If his heart health was at stake, wasn't it a bad idea to go somewhere where he was all alone and couldn't even call 911 if he was having a health crisis? Then spend hours outside shoveling snow and walking uphill?

He stood at the kitchen counter, eating a bland dinner of canned stew right out of the saucepan, along with a few slices of whole wheat toast and an apple for dessert. He was eating for sustenance and to have something to do, not necessarily for pleasure. It was liberating, but depressing, too. The things that he used to enjoy and look forward to were dwindling rapidly.

The wind had picked up outside. He looked out the kitchen window and realized that he could make out the vague shapes of trees, even though it was well past sunset. Luca guessed the clouds must have parted and the moon was out.

He cleaned up his dishes, put on his coat and hat, and stepped outside into the frigid night. He looked up and was marveled at what he saw.

The stars were breathtaking. He hadn't seen so many stars since his trip to Alaska, and even then, it wasn't as magnificent as this. The Milky Way materialized in front of his eyes the longer he stared at the expanse of sky: a collection of stars so abundant they resembled a hazy, sparkling cloud from horizon to horizon.

"Oh my god," Luca whispered. Tears stung his eyes as goosebumps covered the top of his scalp.

The moon was half full and luminous, casting a cool light on the landscape. He remained still, fixated on the sky. A tiny bright dot glided silently and steadily across the sky—a satellite. He hadn't seen one of those in a long time.

An owl hooted nearby. The breeze picked up. His eyeballs became sticky from the freezing cold.

He wished Laura could see this. He wanted to share this moment with her, to put his arms around her, to smell her hair. She mattered so much to him. She and Jordan were everything to him.

Everything.

How had he not known that before now?

*

Luca went to sleep easily but woke abruptly in the middle of the night.

He lay still, listening. The cabin was dead silent. He didn't know if his brain had alerted him to something while he slept or if he was just having one of his annoying bouts of wakefulness and insomnia. He pondered getting out of bed to investigate whether there was anything amiss, but he felt too warm and comfortable under the heavy covers.

He debated with himself a few more minutes and decided that if anything, he should probably get up and throw a few more logs on the fire.

He picked up his phone off the nightstand.

2:22 a.m.

He'd been asleep for about four and a half hours straight. Not bad. Longer than his usual two or three at a time.

He wrapped the comforter around his shoulders and went up to the bedroom window that looked out the front of the cabin onto the porch. He scanned the trees and the dark driveway and didn't see anything. Then he went into the kitchen to look out the back window, behind the cabin and up the hill into the forest.

There was an odd light shining from within the trees, maybe a hundred feet or so from the cabin.

It was odd because it wasn't projecting a beam, it was just a pale, yellow light, as if it was coming from an incandescent low-watt bulb. It was round and approximately the size of a basketball, but had no visible boundaries the way a bulb would.

There were no structures or houses up the slope from the cabin. There was no reason for there to be a light there, nor any electrical appliance.

Was there someone out there in the woods with some sort of lamp, watching the cabin?

Luca watched the light for several minutes to see if it would move or change. It didn't. He walked to side door and made sure it was locked, then looked out the windowpane. He couldn't make out where his snowmobile was; it was too dark. If someone had driven up while he'd slept, he didn't see any evidence of it.

He went back to the kitchen window and unlatched it and then opened it several inches and yelled out.

"HEY, WHO'S THERE? HELLO?"

The light didn't move or even flicker. Luca squinted, trying to make out how far up off the ground the light was or if there was a human shape nearby. All he saw were the trees and the light.

"HEY!" Luca shouted louder. "Who's there? I see your light. What are you doing?"

No answer came from the dark. The light hovered between the branches, unchanged.

Without a flashlight, it was a waste of time for Luca to explore outside now. He wouldn't be able to see much of anything besides the light, and snowshoeing around the trees blind seemed risky. The best course of action, Luca thought, was to sit on the couch and wait. And watch.

*

Luca eventually fell asleep after an hour of keeping vigil watching the unmoving, unchanging light through the window.

When he woke, it was already dawn. Since the sun was rising behind the long mountain range the property flanked, it would be another three hours before sunlight would brighten the tops of the trees, the driveway, and the valley below. Glancing outside the windows he didn't see anything unusual, but it was hard to tell since the light was flat and shadowy. He'd have to go out there and look closer to be sure.

Coffee can wait, he thought.

He got dressed and put on snowshoes. He clomped through the fresh powder that had accumulated in recent days and noted that other than his snowshoe prints on the driveway, he saw a few more rabbit tracks. He scanned the snowdrifts behind the cabin and up into the trees and approached the area where he estimated he had observed the light. His legs sunk down despite the snowshoes, almost up to his knees in spots.

There were no tracks at all where the light had shone. There was no sign that the snow from the last few days had been disturbed since it fell. He turned around and looked back at the cabin, still enshrouded in early-morning winter shadow, and noted that he was in direct line of sight of the kitchen window. Could the light have been in a different location, perhaps higher up the slope, he wondered?

He continued upward, just in case, much further above where he would been able to see from the window. Again, there was no sign that the ground had been disturbed.

"What the hell?" he murmured to himself. He held onto the trunk of a fir tree to keep his balance on the steep slope, catching his breath. He *had* seen a light, hadn't he? What could it have been, other than a light of some sort? Fire? A reflection?

His head felt funny. Luca sensed a faint vibration behind his eyes and then vertigo. Anxious that he'd pass out, he gulped a couple of deep breaths and bent over to allow more blood to flow to his head.

I've got low blood sugar or something, he thought. *Or I'm sleep deprived and delirious.*

After a few minutes, he recovered enough to forge back down the slope but in a different direction, just to cover more ground and make sure he didn't miss anything. Nothing caught his attention there, either.

Odd as it was that there were no tracks, he was relieved. The thought that someone had been surveying the cabin or stalking him creeped him out. He'd been imagining all kinds of scenarios last night. The first scenario was that someone had walked up the driveway (since he hadn't seen or heard any snowmobiles) with the intention of taking shelter or squatting in the cabin. Except why not just do that in the bigger house below? Either way, they'd have to break in.

Or that it was a hunter, tracking an animal or just moving about. He didn't know much about hunting but thought this was probably unlikely in the middle of the night.

It also occurred to him that Shane may have decided to check up on him. But if Shane needed to get a hold of him—because Laura called with some type of emergency—wouldn't he just knock on the door instead of standing still in the woods with a lamp at 2 a.m., watching the cabin like a psychopath?

Regardless, none of these theories held up now because they all required evidence of tracks or footprints, and he didn't see any.

Something was eating away at him, though. He didn't know if the light had been a hallucination or a sign, but something didn't feel right. Perhaps Laura did need to get a hold of him because something really bad had happened with Jordan.

By the time he was back in the kitchen putting the kettle on for coffee, he'd formulated a plan. He would snowmobile down to the main house, check around to see if there had been any human activity down there, and then follow the tracks he and Shane made with their snowmobiles, and ride back to the parking area. He'd bring his phone to check if there had been any messages from Laura.

He wouldn't linger or use it as an excuse to break his technology-free and work-free retreat. He'd just make sure he didn't have any urgent messages. That's all.

You're so weak.

Why, because I need a time out to make sure everything is okay? I'm not being weak, I'm being cautious.

Sure you are.

I'm just making sure there isn't something I'm missing or need to pay attention to. This isn't some excuse!

What if it is an excuse? Why can't you follow through on what you said you'd do? Because you're weak.

Was he being weak? Because he was bored and slightly depressed and wanted to go back to his routine? Was that it?

Then another thought occurred to him.

That he was a little scared. That this place was getting to him.

He leaned against the kitchen counter, sipped the hot coffee, and scoffed. *No. I'm not scared. Scared of what?*

Good question.

He got his phone out of the bedroom where it was plugged into the outlet and checked that it had a full charge. He made himself an extra-large bowl of oatmeal to get him through the morning and then filled up his insulated metal bottle with tap water to take with him.

He was going to do something proactive and rational. *Yes,* he thought, *this is a good plan. I'm going to snowmobile back down to the car where there's service and check my messages. If there aren't any, I'll come right back. No big deal.*

He went from indecisive and down on himself to feeling more upbeat and purposeful than he had in days.

*

The plan fell apart because the snowmobile wouldn't start.

He had brushed off the snow, released the engine kill button as Shane had instructed, turned the key to the ON position, pulled the choke, and yanked the pull cord. It made a quick chuk-chuk-chuk sound but didn't start the motor. He tried again several times before giving up. Each time he yanked the pull cord, he did it slower and slower as the strength in his arm and shoulder drained and he felt a cramp about to radiate in his bicep.

He continued to straddle the machine, running through his mind what he could or should do. He didn't know much about the workings of large engines—let alone small ones. Shane's instructions were simple and clear: engine kill button, key on, choke pulled, yank on pull cord. The gas tank indicator did indeed show that the thing had close to a full tank, as Shane had promised. Since it had a pull start, there was no battery, so that wasn't it. It had to be something else.

I should have asked Shane to come and check up on me after a week. At least I could have asked him to call Laura and see if everything was ok.

Luca did a mental calculation of how far the cabin was the from the Jeep. It had taken, what—a half an hour to snowmobile here? Less? Not in a straight line, and not as fast as a car on asphalt. Maybe three miles? He could snowshoe that distance and back, couldn't he? It'd be a tough six-mile snowshoe, though, with some hills and uneven terrain. He wasn't in the mood to do that. Then again, maybe he wouldn't need to. Maybe he'd get lucky and run into someone a mile or less down the road and they could help him out, figure out how to get the snowmobile started, or make the call to Shane for him if they were headed into town. It was a possibility.

Luca groaned in frustration.

"Thanks for providing your clients with a unreliable snowmobile, asshole!" Luca shouted into the wind. "Really fucking smart!"

The last thing Luca wanted to do today was manage this situation. The worst-case scenario was that he'd stay here as planned and wait for Shane to show up on the afternoon of the 20th.

But that was more than a week away.

"Fuck, fuck, fuck!"

He dismounted and slapped the seat of the machine with his gloved hand before making his way back to the cabin to regroup, warm up, and figure out what he was going to do.

*

He didn't plan on taking a nap, but the lack of a good night's sleep and his recent, long snowshoeing treks had suddenly caught up with him. His glutes and hamstrings were sore and tight. The low-level headache he'd had since his first night here suddenly flared to a tight, nauseating band that started behind his eyes and ran back behind his ears. He thought about making himself more coffee, then opted to drink the last of the beer. Within fifteen minutes, he was hit with a wave of fatigue. The disappointment of not being able to start the snowmobile further drained Luca's resolve, and he opted to lie down and close his eyes for a few minutes. He fell asleep instantly.

He dreamed that he began walking back to his car, but he wasn't alone. Something was following him. Something he couldn't see, but could sense. Perhaps an animal. Each time he turned around, he'd catch glimpses of it darting back into the trees. A formless shadow that would disappear as soon as he caught sight of it. He shouted at it, daring it to come closer, inviting it to show itself. It evaded him—coy and sinister.

In the dream, he didn't sense that he felt fear; he sensed frustration. The kind one might feel in a dream about forgetting a locker combination at school. Or in a dream where the numbers on a cell phone are mixed up or not responding to touch.

It was the frustration of having the right information but being unable to access it.

He woke up and was again disoriented for a few seconds, not sure where he was or what day it was. His mouth was dry and his arms and legs felt shaky. He felt utterly drained despite having just napped. He stared out the window at the intensely blue sky and the golden light that was now touching the tops of the trees in front of the cabin.

He had no desire to go anywhere or accomplish anything. He didn't even want to get up off the couch.

The tendrils of the stalker dream clung to his memory banks for a while longer. He pondered what it might have meant. Perhaps it reflected his desire to connect with Laura, but being unable to? Or maybe it was about how he'd been dogged by the weird phenomenon of the mysterious light and then thwarted by an inoperable engine. Either way, the dream left him feeling bleak.

What if Shane doesn't show up on the 20th like he said he would? I can't stay here forever waiting for him. I'll have to hike out to the car. Not today. It's already too late in the day.

Eventually, Luca forced himself to take a shower, shave, and put on a clean shirt and jeans. He needed to shake this sticky film of gloom that had descended on him. He made himself some tea and added more wood to the fire, appreciating that he was able to keep it lit because of the thick pile of embers that had formed at the bottom of the stove.

He tried to read more, but it was no use. He wasn't engaged in the story. His eyes would wander from the page to around the cabin, to the fire, out the window to the boughs of evergreen swaying in the breeze outside, to the sky, and then back to the fire.

I don't know what I'm doing here. Why did I come here?

He felt detached from the person he was just a week ago, when he'd been planning this getaway. That version of Luca was much more optimistic, perhaps even naïve to the reality of what this two weeks would be like. That version of Luca had the idea that all he needed was to do something radically different in order to *get back to himself.*

Who was the person he was trying to get back to?

He'd always been someone who worked hard and cared about the work he was doing. He'd always been someone who gave just a little too much because he didn't want to let anyone down, especially the people who worked for him and with him. He put in 100-hour workweeks. His schedule meant that he missed nearly all of Jordan's parent-teacher conferences in middle school and couldn't be in the stands for Jordan's state championship football games last year. When Jordan was an infant, he tried to juggle being a supportive husband and father with his burgeoning career, but it wasn't easy. He told himself that he was doing his best to be a provider, and that's why he couldn't always be there when Laura was exhausted and pleaded for him to be home more because she needed help. She needed *him.*

You failed the most important people in your life.

Did he fail them?

His son was a teenager and would soon be going away to college. He was an intelligent, kind, responsible kid. Luca was proud of him. He just wasn't sure how much of that was Laura's influence or his. He could count on one hand the number of times he took his son camping or sailing, or took him to see a movie, or had a heart-to-heart talk with him. Sometimes he'd help him with homework. And yes, they went on a few family vacations over the years—but that wasn't the same as really connecting as father and son.

Laura loved being a mom and was more than happy to make that her full-time job. At least, that's what he assumed. He'd never actually asked her if she wanted to pursue something more for herself, some creative field of study or professional outlet for her passion for social justice. Their conversations usually centered around schedules, to-do lists, Jordan, and Luca's work.

Yes, see? You are a shitty father and a shittier husband.

Was that true?

This was the disconnect. This was the central issue in Luca's mind: that just a week ago, he wasn't questioning the value of his choices. He wasn't asking himself if his family loved and admired him. He was just questioning whether or not he knew how to really relax.

It all seemed laughable now.

Luca gazed at the tall blue spruce that grew closest to the cabin. The tree's branches swayed almost imperceptibly. He thought about how many winters the tree had lived through up on this mountain. Twenty? Fifty? A hundred? Was this tree alive when he was a young boy, walking to school with his younger brother Frank in Newark? Or when he met Laura, during his senior year of college at SUNY? Was it alive when his grandparents met in Italy before the rise of fascism and Mussolini?

The tree would likely outlive him, unless it got burned up in a wildfire. Or he froze or starved to death out here.

Getting real morbid there, old man.

Luca snorted. Yes, he was. He was imagining all sorts of morbid scenarios. Wife leaving him, company letting him go. Perhaps he imagined the light in the woods, too. *Had* the light in the woods been his imagination? It didn't even seem like that had happened thirteen hours ago. It felt like it happened a year ago.

The sun was setting already. The days were so short this time of year.

He got up, stretched, jogged in place. Took deep, invigorating breaths. He felt his hunger return. He went to the kitchen to see what he had left to eat.

A dozen cans were lined up against the backsplash, along with what was left of the bags of pasta and a couple of jars of sauce. Stews and soups, mostly. A can of pork and beans.

And a single can of SpaghettiOs.

He picked up the can and turned it over, smiling to himself. This was his favorite meal when he was a kid. His mom would make it for him for lunch in the summer, when he'd come in from playing outside with the neighbor kids. It was always for lunch, never for dinner, because his father "didn't eat outta cans." Dinner always had to be something his mother cooked from scratch.

That's why SpaghettiOs tasted so good to him. It was different than the meals his mom cooked. It was tangy, salty, and with the fun circular noodle shapes through which he liked to stick his tongue.

This was the first time he'd seen a SpaghettiOs can in what— 40 years? He didn't even know they still made them until he went shopping for groceries at the market in Ridgway. He bought the can out of a sense of nostalgia and wanting to reconnect to more carefree days, he supposed.

He grabbed the can opener out of the drawer, punctured the can, and started turning the handle. As the top of the can was cut away, the smell of the Romano cheese-infused tomato sauce wafted up to his nose.

Luca's guts were stirred by an old memory:

The whirring of an electric can opener. The can of SpaghettiOs going round and round. Standing on a chair next to the stove, taking the can and dumping the contents into a sauce pan.

Something about the stove not working. Not knowing why. What was wrong with the stove?

The sweet, sickly smell of gas.

His father's booming voice, "WHAT THE HELL DO YOU THINK YOU'RE DOING?" Then his father's fist knocking him off the chair.

The tight grip of fear.

No. More like terror.

"YOU'RE GONNA BURN THE HOUSE DOWN YOU IDIOT!"

Again, Luca wondered if this was a real memory or something he'd seen in a movie, or what. Did this happen to him? If so, when did this happen?

Mimicking what he was remembering, he dumped the contents of the can into the saucepan he set out on the stove. Then he turned the knob on the burner, lifted the pan and flicked the Bic lighter, moving it close to the burner. Blue, soft flames appeared under the saucepan.

An image was gelling. The stove didn't work because he hadn't known how to light the gas. Yes! That's right. His parents weren't home and that's why he was trying to make himself his favorite meal, standing on a chair next to the stove without anyone to help him.

He stirred the pasta and sauce, and his vision softened as he tried to remember more details. His sense was that he had been alone at home, which means that neither his parents nor his brother—who was five years younger—were around.

There it was, this polaroid-filter memory.

His father told him he was driving his mother to the hospital to have the baby and that he was to STAY PUT until he—or they— got home. Luca complied, but they were gone far too long. It was getting dark, he was getting hungry and scared. Really scared.

What if they aren't coming home? He remembered thinking.

He'd gotten in trouble because he didn't STAY PUT and had tried to cook himself something to eat without knowing how to work the stove. The whole thing felt so unfair to him, he remembered now. Deeply unfair. It also planted a seed in him that had stayed buried and ungerminated, until now.

"Wow," Luca whispered, watching as bubbles formed at the edges of the bright orange liquid and in between the white, starchy o's. "I can't believe I didn't remember that until now."

He thought about Jordan at that age and couldn't imagine leaving him home alone, or being angry at him because he'd gotten hungry and scared, let alone knocking him down to the ground and calling him an idiot.

His heart burst with a wave of tenderness for the little boy he was then, and tears filled his eyes.

Still pondering what happened to him so long ago, he found a set of placemats in one of the drawers, along with some paper napkins. He set out a plate, a bowl, and a spoon. He toasted two slices of bread and spread out a good-size glob of margarine on each one, placing it on the plate next to the bowl. Then he made a hot cup of tea with some honey and put it next to his plate. Last, he poured the entire can of heated SpaghettiOs into the bowl before sitting down to eat.

I may not be perfect, but I sure as hell am nothing like my father, Luca thought as he bit into the buttery toast with a satisfying crunch.

*

The next morning, he felt much less sore and much more energetic. He'd slept well, only waking up once in the middle of the night, and then falling right back to sleep until about 6 a.m.

He made himself two peanut butter and jelly sandwiches and filled the now-empty plastic gallon jug that had held spring water with tap well water, then stuffed the food and his fully-charged cellphone into the pockets of his parka. He dressed in three layers: a sweat-wicking undershirt, a fleece pullover, and the parka. He also put on gloves, a knit hat, and stuffed his gaiter in the inner pocket in case it got windy later.

As soon as it was light enough outside, he went out to try to start the snowmobile but had no luck with it. *Just as well,* he thought, and put on the snowshoes.

He made one last run-through of his mental checklist: phone, wallet, car keys, food, water. Check.

He started down the driveway, the previous day's determination and sense of purpose revving back up and quickening his stride. It was another clear, blue day and the air was calm and crisp. If he had to guess, he'd say it was 15 degrees Fahrenheit. Cold enough to freeze the snot from the base of his nostrils if he hadn't brought some napkins to wipe it off first.

The driveway was steepest at the top, then it made two hairpin turns, then gradually the angle lessened until he was almost out of the trees and coming up on the main house. Large clumps of snow from the recent storm slid off the branches of trees and smacked the ground as he clomped past.

At the last turn, something darted in his peripheral vision. It disappeared behind a tree 50 feet ahead of him and to the right.

Something black. And furry. And big.

He stood still for a moment, his eyes scanning in between the tree trunks, not seeing anything. Not wanting to miss whatever it was, he jogged down to where he'd seen the thing cross the driveway.

The pawprints were huge. His eyes followed them to where they ended. He turned his body in that direction, and gasped as he locked eyes with the creature.

A mountain lion.

Or some kind of big cat. It was all black with piercing, golden yellow eyes. Its fuzzy tail hung low to the ground and was at least three feet long. Its head was turned toward him, watching, waiting.

Luca held his breath. He willed the cat to *not move.*

"Are you real?" Luca whispered, his complete attention on the animal. "You're magnificent."

The cat blinked once, slowly, then turned its head forward and slinked away into the forest. Luca watched it for several minutes as it made its way up the hill, graceful and sleek.

Luca didn't know mountain lions could be black. He wondered if what he saw was actually a jaguar or panther. But here, in Colorado?

"Sure, because why not? This has been the week of weird," he muttered.

Once he could no longer see the cat, he reluctantly continued down the driveway. He noted as he approached the main house that there was no sign that anyone had been around in the last day or two since it snowed. His tracks were the only ones he saw.

He continued in the direction of the car, retracing the route he and Shane had snowmobiled. Eventually, the snowmobile tracks diverged, an older one into the woods and fresher ones following the main road. The older ones must have been where he and Shane had exited the woods from their shortcut. He thought for a second, then decided to play it safe and follow the older tracks, in case the main road was a longer route or led him away from where he needed to go. He didn't want to dick around today with new adventures. It was too cold and he had stuff to do.

Fortunately, the trees had served to block most of the snow that had fallen, and he was able to follow the snowmobile tracks easily up and over and out the other side of the hill. He was starting to sweat from his effort and decided to take off his parka and tie it around his waist. The Colorado winter sun was like a microwave at this altitude, as well as blinding and intense, due to its lower path in the winter sky. He tolerated the chill of the shade to keep himself from sweating too much in the sunshine.

Finally, in the distance, he saw the glimmer of vehicles at the parking area. Checking his phone, however, he saw that it still registered NO SERVICE.

Still blocked by the mountain, probably, Luca concluded.

He saw that a couple more vehicles had parked next to his since he'd arrived almost a week ago. His Jeep was covered in snow. The parking lot had been plowed, and the berms along the edges were taller.

The snowmobile path in and out of the parking area had created a smooth, hard surface that made the last few yards of snowshoeing much easier. He bent down, unbuckled the straps and removed the snowshoes off his boots, holding them in his left, gloved hand. He felt instantly lighter and less constricted, but without the snowshoes his boots punched a few inches down into the snowpack.

He jumped a little when his phone started dinging with text message alerts. A wave of familiar, pleasant anticipation washed over him. He took his gloves off with his teeth and brought the phone out of his pocket and close to his face to read it.

A text from Laura:

Hey, are you on your phone when you're not supposed to be? LOL. Just a note to say I love you and I'm thinking about you. Hopefully you're reading this at the end of your solo retreat and you're safe and on your way home. Miss you! See you soon.

Luca whooped out a "Yes!" and laughed with relief.

Back at the Jeep, he dropped the snowshoes, took off his other glove and scrolled through the "recents" in his phone app. He found the entry with a 970 prefix—the local area code—and tapped it.

He looked around and saw two snowmobiles approaching over the hill from the direction he'd just come. Above him, multiple contrails crisscrossed the horizon where planes had recently carried hundreds of people across thousands of miles. Chimney smoke rose from a sprawling ranch house a quarter of a mile down the road, in the direction of Ridgway.

He heard the distant barking of a dog.

And relaxed into the silence in between the sounds.

The signal connected after a few seconds and the line started ringing.

Luca closed his eyes and waited patiently for Shane to answer his phone.

DOG

"Unfortunately, there can be no doubt that man is, on the whole, less good than he imagines himself or wants to be." — C.G. Jung, *Psychology and Religion* (1938)

In her dream, it was dark, and the snow was blowing sideways as she hunched against the wind. She sensed the irregular shapes of pines and conifers flanking her as she trudged through the ankle-deep drifts. She was following a whimpering sound that shifted directions as soon as she closed in on it. It was the whimpering of a dog.

"Where are you? Come here!" she shouted into the wind.

The dog's whining became louder and more insistent. Yet, she couldn't quite pinpoint where the sound was coming from.

She stumbled over twigs and rocks that were buried in snow. Each time she thought she was getting closer, she fell and had to pick herself up again. Her hands were numb. She wasn't wearing gloves.

Suddenly a pair of headlights pierced the tree branches and the flurry of wet flakes. Relief swept over her. The road was just ahead, maybe another fifty feet. She made her way forward until she was out of the forest and standing on the side of the road, squinting at the headlights.

The vehicle approached slowly from the opposite side of the road from where she stood. Then it stopped. Windshield wipers pivoted on slow speed back and forth, smearing the snow into a reflective, slushy glaze she couldn't see through.

The interior of the car was dark. She could make out a dark shape in the driver's seat but not any other features. She approached the driver's side and waved the car away.

"No! Don't stop! Keep driving!" She shouted, but her voice sounded stifled, far away, as if she was yelling from underneath a layer of blanket. The car continued to idle, the worn-out wiper blades bouncing across the windshield. *Squeek wonnng. Squeek wonnng.*

"Hey! Do you hear me?" She moved forward and rapped on the driver's side window with her frozen, raw knuckles. She couldn't feel her hands.

Three seconds later, the window rolled down. A pale face looked up at her with a mixture of concern and exhaustion.

She took a step backward.

She was looking at her own face! Was it a reflection? A wave of dizziness overtook her as her expression was reflected back to her.

Suddenly the spell was broken and she felt herself lift out of the dream as if swimming up from the depths of a dark ocean, reaching for breath, reaching for the light. She took a deep gasp of air, then snapped into consciousness.

Her eyes opened and she heard the real-world sound of the wind rattling the house. The whimpering was clear and close now, within a couple of feet of her head. She rolled over and flung her arm over the side of her bed.

The dog's wet nose brushed up against her forearm.

"It's okay," she whispered. "You're safe. Everything is going to be okay."

*

Two Weeks Earlier
8:35 am

Bev reached the top of the hill and stopped to enjoy the view. There was a small break in the 20-foot-tall piñons that lined the gravel road, and a small grassy meadow allowed her to see several miles down valley, toward the Cimarron Range of the San Juan mountains. The air was brisk, just above freezing, and the sun was warm and friendly on her face.

This was her favorite time of the day, before the flow of on-line orders and emails and hours spent at the kitchen counter, measuring and mixing. This was her time to daydream or make plans, or just listen to sounds of the landscape.

Flocks of crows flew diagonally across field of vision, close enough to the top of the trees that she could hear their wings making a pleasant *shoop shoop shoop* sound. Chickadees screeched out a whistle in between their *chicka-dee-dee-dee* song. A breeze created a gentle rustling sound as it passed through the trees.

In between these sounds, there was almost complete silence. Cars were rare on this stretch of road this time of the morning, especially since the road dead ended a half mile west. Later in the day, she might see a neighbor driving past with a wave, or the postal carrier or the UPS truck.

Farther east toward the main county road she heard someone's dog barking rhythmically. *Ark! Ark! Ark!* She'd hear that same bark late in the evenings and early in the mornings if she left her bedroom window open a little bit, which she did most nights, for fresh air and to keep the room cool. Sometimes it'd be barking at 2 o'clock in the morning. *Ark! Ark! Ark!* Sometimes more insistently, like it was warning something away.

She wondered why the dog kept barking so much. Coyotes? Boredom? A bad temperament? Why didn't the owners bring the dog in? Weren't they bothered by all that barking? If she could hear it all the way over here, surely they must hear it much better if it's yapping under their windows.

Bev didn't know much about her neighbors yet since she had just moved into her house a few weeks ago. She identified them by the vehicles they drove. There was the man who appeared to be in his 50s who drove an older dark red truck with a dented tailgate. She imagined he was a contractor of some kind because he had a toolbox in the bed of the truck, although what kind of contractor, she couldn't be sure. The truck didn't have any signs on it. She'd seen his truck pulling into the driveway closest to her house, a few hundred feet west of her driveway.

Her neighbors farther west on her road were more of a mystery. On one of her drives back from town, she passed a blue Jeep wrangler. The driver was a blond woman who appeared to be in her mid-30s.

Bev continued downhill. She put her hand in her jacket pocket, felt around for the wadded tissue and brought it up to her nose. She picked up the pace, wanting to get in a little more distance today and a little more exercise before she had to turn around. She'd walk another 20 minutes before turning back.

She wished she could just keep walking for hours, until the road ran out or she got tired and hungry and had to go back. It felt so good to be outside, breathing the clean air and listening to the jibber-jabber of the birds. But she didn't linger, because she felt a vague pull toward home, where she had orders to fill and more soap to make.

She enjoyed her work and knew she was fortunate to have a successful home-based business. For years, her struggle had been to find the right balance between spending time in nature, and time working in front of the computer or in the shop. If orders weren't coming in for some reason, whether it was the slow season after January or because she hadn't invested enough in marketing, she felt uneasy and mildly depressed. Keeping busy kept her from feeling in limbo or like a nobody. When she lived in Denver, and work was slow, she would meet friends for coffee or take on a home improvement project. Inevitably, right before she began to wonder if she should continue with her business, orders would pick up and she'd be back to making batch after batch of soap and packaging orders to take to the post office.

Before long, the cycle would begin anew and she would start to feel anxious and discontent, longing for more time outside, more time in nature, more time spent hiking. When she lived in Denver she only had time to go up to the mountains on weekends when she wasn't busy with work. Most of her walks in Denver were around the suburban neighborhoods that interconnected and went on for miles. Nature there was a greenbelt with planted cottonwoods or ash trees and manicured lawns. To get to wilder nature, she'd had to get in the car and drive at least 40 minutes.

Here she could just walk out her front door and be in an environment that hadn't been manicured or sprayed with Roundup or swept with a leaf blower. She could see mountains up close and all around. She could breathe air that smelled of pine and sage instead of car exhaust and asphalt.

One problem solved, another one created, she thought. Because now, sitting inside all day working seemed like a waste of a perfectly lovely day.

She looked at her iPhone and saw that it was already 9:15 am.

Crap. Lounged around too long on this morning's walk. Have to get a move on. She turned around and started making her way back up towards the long hill, at the crest of which would be a rabbitbrush and grassy meadow, and then her driveway, another half mile up.

She noticed something at the crest of the hill. A small, dark shape. Was it a deer? It wasn't moving, but she could tell it was an animal of some kind. A bear? She couldn't see it clearly enough yet to know what it was, and from this distance she didn't think she was in any danger if it was a bear.

She had seen bears on the mesa before, during her summer trips to the area when she visited her friend Colleen. They were common here, but mostly stayed away from humans except to raid their trash cans, or, on the rare occasion, open car doors to rummage for snacks.

The animal started moving at a quick pace down the hill toward her.

She stopped and squinted to clear her vision and figure out what it was. It wasn't making a sound and it was too small and nimble and fast to be a bear. Her brain was trying to make sense of the shape, the gait, and the size.

And then she realized what it was.

A dog. A black dog. It wasn't barking or making any sort of sound as it made its way down the hill, in a straight line right toward her. She didn't see anyone or anything else behind it. No owner, no car, no one to call it back.

"Fucking hell."

This was worse than a bear. A bear would probably catch a glimpse of her and saunter off or run away. If you happen to walk past as they were filling their mouth with acorns, they'd likely just keep chewing as long as you kept your distance.

But a dog. Dogs were fine as long as they were on a leash or behind a fence or sitting calmly in front of their owner. Some dogs were adorable and smart. Her dog, Raven, for example. Calm, cuddly, gentle. Not at all aggressive. A trusted companion.

Untethered, unrestrained, loose dogs were a whole other category in her mind.

A dog running toward her without an owner in sight was terrifying to her.

She took a deep breath. The dog advanced. She weighed her options.

Stand and wait? Run away from it and into the woods? Run *toward* it?

"Hey!" she shouted as loud as she could. "No! Stay!"

The dog hesitated and slowed a bit, then skidded to a stop.

She took one step forward. Then another.

"Go home! Go on!"

She wanted to sound intimidating despite feeling scared. It wasn't difficult. She was getting pissed. God damnit, don't people fence their dogs around here? She looked around for some bigger rocks that she could throw at the dog, just in case it started coming at her again and found a nice round one the size of an apple. She picked it up and started walking toward the dog.

She got close enough to see that it was a medium-sized dog, with a long coat, perhaps a cross between a black lab and a border collie. It continued to stand still without taking its eyes off her. Then it hunched down a bit the way border collies do when herding sheep, thrusting its neck forward. Like it was getting ready to pounce. Or chase.

Bev held her breath for a few seconds. Her heart was pounding and she could feel the bile from the morning's coffee spill up into the back of her throat.

No, no, no, no, NO!

A clammy sensation made its way down Bev's spine. It was déjà vu.

When she lived in Denver, she'd go jogging along the greenbelt sometimes in the mornings. The concrete path meandered through several neighborhoods. One of the fenced yards along the path had a dog that would snarl and bark and throw himself at the weathered and splintered fence that separated her from it.

She caught glimpses of it through the gaps in between the cedar slats as she ran by. Short-haired, muddy brown, and stocky. Every time she passed that yard, she would brace herself, and every time she'd still be startled by the sudden scratching and growling.

The fence bulged in the places the dog scratched and jumped. She'd wonder, each time she jogged past, how long it would hold before giving way, and what the dog might do when it got out. The two-story house had peeling paint and torn and crooked window screens. She imagined they probably left their dog out in the yard most of the time.

Despite the situation, she didn't change her route. It would have meant bypassing the green belt altogether and jogging next to the busy road. So she just braced herself and breathed through it, telling herself that it was just one of those unpleasantries one has to tolerate.

One morning, she was lost in a podcast and didn't see the dog lying on the grass next to his yard (and his broken fence) until it was too late.

It was definitely the same dog who'd been snarling at her from behind a fence all those times. Same short, brown fur. Same general largish build. Same ugly, black-lined mouth that she saw sticking through the gaps in the fence.

Momentarily confused, she just kept running forward. Why was he out of his yard? Was there someone there with him? Before she could react and change her direction, the dog turned his head, made eye contact with her, and stood up. Moments later, he careened toward her in complete silence.

He fell on her just as she threw her arms up to protect her face.

She screamed and kicked at the beast for what felt like several minutes before a woman in one of the houses next to the green-belt ran out to help her.

She sustained scratches and shallow bites on her leg and arm, but nothing that needed stitches. She filed a report with the police. Animal control impounded the dog and cited the owner, but past that, she didn't know if they had fixed their fence or kept their dog inside.

She never ran down that greenbelt again.

But all those feelings, all that terror, came rushing back as she faced the black dog with a rock in her hand, wishing she'd brought bear spray on this walk. She had no reason to think it was aggressive, necessarily. Not yet. He wasn't barking or growling. He looked intensely focused, though.

"Where did you come from, huh?" She tried to keep her tone assertive.

The dog took a step backward and turned its head to the side, either to signal his acquiescence or plan an escape route. Her tone and stance seemed to be working.

"Are you friendly?" The dog started to pant and swish his tail in short, slow arcs. His eyes softened and squinted. She was close enough now that she could see it had a small white patch of fur on its chest.

"Where's your home?" She put the rock in her pocket and squatted down, holding her hand out in a friendly gesture.

The dog turned around abruptly and started walking back up the hill. Bev followed behind, picking up her pace so she could see where it went. As she crested the top, she could see that it stopped and turned around up ahead, looking back in her direction. When it spotted her, it continued running down the road and made a left turn into a long, dirt driveway. Ok, it looked like it was her neighbor's dog. The man with the red pickup. His driveway was long enough that she couldn't see his house from the road.

By the time she was close enough to see the full length down the driveway before it curved, the dog was gone. No cars, no dogs, no people. She didn't realize until she was within sight of her own house, how tense she had gotten. She jogged the rest of the distance to her front door.

When she walked inside her house Raven came running to greet her. Raven was a rescue dog, a small, short-haired black dog that looked like it had a little bit of rat terrier, a little bit of pointer and a little bit of Lab mixed together. Her fur was smooth and silky, and she had a patch of grey and white marbling around her chest.

Bev squatted down to rub Raven behind the ears and let out a long sigh. She hadn't taken Raven on a walk this morning, preferring the solitude and wanting to have a brisker walk that would have frustrated Raven's desire to sniff every bush and clump of grass along the culvert. Now she was particularly glad she didn't. Raven had a way of attracting the attention of off-leash dogs. But not in a good way. Her body language must be offensive to those dogs because even when people she meets on the trail let her know their dog is "friendly", their dog inevitably growls or snaps at Raven.

Bev was sure this wasn't helping Raven and was probably contributing to her anxiety and fear around unleashed dogs. For this reason, and because Raven wasn't very good at recall commands, Bev never walked her without a leash.

She wondered what would have happened if the dog she encountered just now had spotted Raven.

A pang of worry came over her. She had walked Raven on the road a few times since she had moved into the house, but she'd never seen that black dog before today. Was it a fluke? Was the dog usually fenced in, but had gotten out today?

What would happen if she took Raven on a walk and encountered the dog again?

No walks with Raven until she figured this out. For now, Raven would probably be fine wandering around the fenced area off the back deck where Bev normally let her out to do her business or just hang out in the sun.

She poured herself another cup of coffee and walked across the driveway and behind her house to her workshop. She laid out the supplies to start another large batch of soap.

She put on some music to cheer herself up and got to work.

*

The sun had just dropped below the western horizon as Bev pulled out of her driveway and turned east toward County Road 1. The shadows intensified and the forest of piñon and juniper turned into a dark mass that stretched west 60 miles upward to the crest of the Uncompahgre Plateau before plunging down to the desert of Paradox Valley, which was a short drive east of Utah.

Ahead and to the south was the Sneffels Range, the longest and tallest contiguous mountain range oriented east and west in the continental United States. That's just one of several trivia tidbits she'd memorized about the mountain range since moving here. She also learned that the entire range, with the exception of Mount Sneffels—the only "fourteener" of the range—was compressed ash from the volcanic explosions that formed the mountains in southwest Colorado. Mount Sneffels was granite that raised upward out of the earth.

She was in love with this mountain range. She loved seeing photos of it, she loved looking at all its moods, from covered in snow in winter to completely exposed in late August, or in between, lightly dusted in white or shrouded in mist or rain clouds. She couldn't get enough.

And now she stared at its shadowy, post-sunset face while driving toward the small town of Ridgway, to her friend Colleen's house, where she had been invited to dinner. Raven sat companionably in the front seat, looking straight ahead, eyes wide open and her nose twitching every now and then when she caught whiff of a deer outside through the car vent.

It was only a little past 5 o'clock but it felt much later, as if she had lost a couple of hours somewhere in the day.

"I feel like I should be getting ready for bed, not going out." She complained to Raven.

Was it always this dark in late November? She didn't remember noticing how short the days were this time of year. If she were back in Denver, she might be headed to the grocery store, or out to meet friends after work for a show or to check out a new restaurant. The darkness there wasn't as noticeable, perhaps because the freeways were lit with a sea of brake lights and the glow of billboards and signs. Trees in front of commercial buildings and offices would be decorated with Christmas lights this time of year, blue and red LED lights coiled around the trunks and branches all the way to the top. Suburban homes would be decorated with giant blow-up Santas and reindeer, icicle lights, pulsing lights, or the twirling projections of stars on the entire façade of a house.

Here, she hadn't seen any holiday lights decorating any of the houses that sparsely dotted the landscape. There were a few brightly decorated homes in the larger town of Montrose, 20 miles north, but not here on the mesa. She supposed no one wanted to bother putting up lights only a few people, if any, would see. Also, many of the houses were second homes that were vacant most of the year. There were also no streetlights anywhere on the mesa, only the occasional reflectors on mailboxes and fence posts. No one lit their driveway, there were no monument signs, and no one had permanent outdoor lights installed. Once in a while, you'd see the warm glow from an upstairs bedroom window or a pair of headlights moving down a hill.

All of this contributed to the dark wildness of the place in the winter compared to the "big city".

She dimmed her brights as a courtesy to a car that approached from the opposite direction. Once the car passed, she immediately clicked them back on. Even so, the lights barely penetrated the surrounding woods and only about 100 feet of road ahead. The drive to Ridgway was seven miles of this, and down several switchbacks to the valley and then another couple miles to town.

Lately, Bev had to force herself to go anywhere after sunset. Maybe it was her reticence to drive in that darkness, or maybe it was her mood. She felt restless, bored, even a little bit depressed some evenings.

When Colleen asked her to dinner, she was relieved. She was spared another evening sitting at home trying to fill the time with reading and TV, neither of which excited her much.

Colleen had been her friend for nearly 20 years. They had met while working at an ad agency in Denver. She moved to Ridgway after meeting her boyfriend Terry at a music festival in Denver. Terry had lived in Ridgway for years and owned and operated an outdoor equipment rental shop in town. Colleen had always wanted to live in the mountains, so she didn't hesitate at all when Terry asked her to relocate. She got a part-time job writing for the local paper and a freelance gig writing grants for a nonprofit back in Denver.

Colleen had campaigned for Bev to move to Ridgway ever since Bev's husband died from a heart attack five years ago. She knew how much Bev loved the area and thought that being closer to the mountains and nature would be good for her. So far, it had been.

She parked in front of Colleen and Terry's two-story stucco house and scooped up Raven so she wouldn't wander off down the unlit street. There were no sidewalks, and the road was unpaved on this side of town. She went up to the gate and let herself into the front yard. The path to the front door was dark, so she took slow, deliberate steps so she wouldn't trip over anything.

"Hey you two," Colleen greeted them at the door. Bev stepped inside, put Raven down and kicked off her shoes.

Colleen was wearing an apron over her jeans and t-shirt. There was a splotch of some type of tomato sauce across the chest, where large graphic drawings of eggplants, leeks and onions decorated the fabric. A stray clump of hair had gotten free of her ponytail and had hooked underneath her chin. She was smiling broadly, hands on hips.

"Chilly tonight. I guess winter is really around the corner."

"It wasn't bad today. It felt rather warm in the sun." Bev watched as Raven made her way toward the kitchen, from where the savory smells of dinner were emanating. "I'm just glad that it's finally normal weather. Well, sort of normal."

"Yeah, that seventy degrees the other day was definitely cray cray."

Bev followed Colleen into the center of house. Terry was sitting on a stool at the kitchen island, sipping from a glass of wine and scrolling through his smartphone.

"Hey Bev. Get you a glass of wine?"

"Sure, that'd be great." Bev straddled one of the stools and positioned herself in front of a plate of appetizers. She popped a cube of cheese into her mouth just as Terry slid a glass of red wine in front of her.

Colleen stirred at a pot of something on the stove and checked the burner setting for something simmering in a large skillet.

"How's life up on the mesa?" Terry put his phone down and leaned down to scratch Raven on the head. "You meet any of your neighbors yet?"

"Well, I haven't spoken with any of them yet, no. I've seen them drive past in their cars. Met one of their dogs today." She examined an olive that was stuffed with something white, probably garlic, before biting into it. "It was just going for a walk. Scared me a little."

"Why'd it scare you? Did it growl at you or something?" Colleen crossed her arms and leaned back against the counter, frowning. She knew about Bev's dog attack from before.

"Just because I didn't know if it was friendly or not. I still don't know. It wouldn't let me get too close."

"Life in the country. People don't pen their dogs in." Terry stopped rubbing Raven's head and went back to his phone. "Especially up there."

"I wouldn't let Raven run around outside by herself outside of your yard, though," Colleen said. "There was a woman up there last year whose little poodle got snatched up by wolves."

"What? There aren't wolves around here. C'mon." Bev chuckled, scratched Raven's head and then and looked up at Colleen. Colleen wasn't smiling.

"I'm dead serious, Bev. I don't know if this was a wolf or a coyote or a dog or what. But I know this woman, she works at the salon. She cut my hair once. Nice lady, totally on the level. She said she was out in front of her house after getting the mail and her little dog was with her, and when she turned around, she saw a big timber wolf type thing run off into the woods with it. It didn't even make a sound. She didn't even hear it coming."

"She was imagining things. It was probably a coyote," Terry said. "Bev is right, there are no wolves here. The closest are up in Wyoming in Yellowstone."

"I don't agree. They were tracking a pack of them up in North Park the other summer. Remember that? They could have made their way down here. Also, what if someone was keeping wolves as pets and one of them got out? It happens, you know."

"Can't explain it. I just know there aren't wolves around here." Terry took a sip of his wine and then turned to Bev and winked as if to say, *I'm going to drive her crazy, watch.*

"They tagged a wolf in the Grand Canyon once. Maybe it wandered up from Mexico. There are wolves down there, you know.

Not the same kind as up in Wyoming, though," Bev said. She looked around for Raven, who had disappeared somewhere in the living room behind her. "Anyway, she's been living here for ten years, and she said she knows what a coyote looks like. She said that was no coyote."

Terry typed something into his phone. He paused, then turned the phone around to show Bev. "What does that look like to you?"

Bev looked at the picture on the screen. It was of a rather large and fluffy coyote, but with a less pointy snout than she recognized. "What's that? Looks like a coyote but stockier."

"It's a coywolf. A hybrid between a coyote and a wolf. Think maybe that's what she saw?"

"Right, so there aren't wolves up here, but coyotes are making babies with them?" Colleen asked.

"I didn't say that. But maybe Bev's theory is better. Someone is keeping a wolf hybrid up on the mesa as a pet and it got out. Happened in the foothills of Denver, you know. Some crazy bat kept a couple of wolf hybrids as pets and let them run around at night, hunting down whatever they could, including her neighbor's cats and dogs."

"Jesus." Bev shook her head.

"This dog you saw," Colleen asked, "it wasn't a wolf, was it?" She winked at Bev.

"No, that's just it. Not a wolf. It looked like some kind of lab border collie mix." She paused, took a sip of her wine. "It just sucks because you know how Raven is around unleashed dogs."

"Can you talk to your neighbor, maybe ask them about the dog?" Terry asked.

"I can't even see the house where the owner lives. It's down a really long driveway. I don't know. Maybe I'll write them a note and stick it in their mailbox."

"I would. People have to have some consideration. Not let their dogs run around willy nilly." Colleen started taking plates out of the cupboard and setting them on the dining table, which was next to the window overlooking their backyard. "Alright, let's eat. I'm hungry."

Terry and Bev took their glasses to the table and Bev helped Colleen put the dishes of food out on the table. There was a pot of vegetable stew and grilled cheese paninis. It looked delicious. Bev felt her stomach growl and slid down into the chair with anticipation of the meal.

Maybe she could write a note to her neighbor, inquire politely about the dog. In fact, she should probably write one to all three of her neighbors since it was nearly impossible to catch them outside or talk with them while they were in their cars. She could introduce herself, offer her email and phone number. She wanted to get off on the right foot at her new home, get to know the people that lived nearby a little bit. How long had they lived there, what did they do for a living? Were they retired? What did they do for fun?

She imagined inviting her neighbors over for a meal or maybe just coffee and dessert. She imagined summer barbeques and interesting conversations on her deck. She imagined having a glass of wine with a woman her age, sharing stories, and laughing about something.

Before moving to the small mountain town of Ridgway, Bev and her late husband Rick lived in an older, suburban neighborhood of Denver in an older, ranch-style house with a good-sized backyard and front lawn. Their neighbors were mostly older than they were at the time, perhaps in their 50s and 60s, some retired and some still doing a 9 to 5. They were friendly but kept to themselves. Bev and Rick would say hi when they'd pass them on their evening walks. They'd be shoveling their driveways in winter or mowing their lawns in the summer. Once in a while, one of them would stop them to talk about some vandalism or home burglary that occurred in the neighborhood. Or they would gossip about which house was going up for sale because someone had died or gotten a divorce. Bev and Rick got invited to a block party once. Otherwise, no grand friendships had been forged.

The few times that Bev visited Colleen and Terry in Ridgway she was impressed at how warm and friendly the locals seemed. Colleen's neighbors would come by to chat in front of their house; and during town events like the 4th of July picnic or the weekly farmer's market, she saw many people visiting and laughing together. They had quite a few friends in town with whom they'd go skiing or hiking, and so, she imagined that when she moved to Ridgway, she'd make friends like that, too. She certainly didn't want to rely on Colleen and Terry for company all the time. She knew that would quickly become tiresome for everyone involved.

She wasn't really expecting that she would make close friendships with her neighbors on her street, but she liked the idea that at least they'd be friendly and help each other out in case anything happened, like if a massive blizzard snowed them in for days at a time. She heard from Colleen that there was a winter a few years ago where three huge weather systems pounded the area with over four feet of snow over the course of a week, pretty much stranding everyone until the snowplows could tackle the secondary roads. Full-time residents with ATVs were able to clear their driveways and some of the county roads. This small town was a lot more neighborly than Denver, partly out of necessity, partly out of the need for human connection since there were relatively fewer people around.

Bev thought about the ATV that was parked in her garage. It came with the house, but Bev hadn't yet figured out how to work it or whether or not it would even turn over. She was planning on having Terry take a look at it for her this week, maybe even put it on his trailer and take it into town for a tune-up. Living alone without her handy husband around was a tremendous pain in the ass, Bev often thought. Sometimes if she couldn't unlock a stuck screw or figure out how to fix something it just wouldn't get fixed. She'd buy a new one instead.

Yes, Rick had certainly been handy. She missed that. She missed not having to worry about things breaking down. She missed their conversations. He always had something thoughtful to say about a book he was reading or about why a friend was acting weird. She liked listening to him read from the psychology journals and magazines he subscribed to. She missed feeling loved and having someone to love. She missed his steady, cheerful companionship.

She had been too busy lately to ponder what winter would be like this year up on the mesa living by herself without close friends and a job to commute to every day. The idea of it was like knowing that a big storm was coming, but not knowing exactly when. Or how to prepare. Just having a vague sense that you'd be cut off, stuck, and it would take work and time to dig out.

"What are you thinking about?" asked Colleen.

"Me? Oh, I dunno. Just daydreaming, sorry. The soup is good. What's new and exciting around town?" Bev tore another chunk of bread and dipped it into her soup before slurping it up with pleasure.

Due to her job, Colleen was on top of all the town's gossip. She was the first to hear when a business was shutting or when someone new and semi-famous was moving into town. She often had a funny story or anecdote to tell about some old coot living off grid who was calling in to the paper to complain about county government again.

Colleen squinted slightly as she leaned forward over her bowl, leaning on her elbows. "You know that Texan that bought those 200 acres north of town I told you about? The one who had been building fences and getting landscaping done bit by bit each summer? The one that built that massive house a few years ago?"

"I remember you telling me about him. What'd he do?"

"He's suing his neighbor now. Apparently back in September some of his neighbor's cattle broke down the fence between their property and trampled up his precious landscaping near his house, crapped all over his driveway, did a bunch of damage. Or so he claims."

Terry snorted quietly and shook his head.

Bev chuckled. She'd heard stories from Colleen about this guy. He was a retired oil executive from Dallas who had been coming to the area for years every summer with his family to ride his Jeep over the mountain passes. He had a reputation around town because he had fought tooth and nail with the county commissioners about the size and location of his house, which barely passed local visual impact ordinances. He was not a likeable person, apparently.

"So now he's pissed off his neighbor and pretty much every person living on that county road. Apparently he's moving here full-time in a few months after he retires. Not a great way to start things off. You know, suing your neighbor."

"Was there really that much damage?"

"I talked with the guy he's suing. Says it barely amounts to a few hundred dollars in shrubs and flowers. Anyway, he doesn't have a leg to stand on. In this county, if you don't want your neighbor's livestock on your property, it's your responsibility to build a proper fence to keep the cattle out, not the rancher's."

"Doesn't sound like a good move," Bev said. "His suing, I mean,"

"It's not," Terry said. "When your neighbors are against you, it can get pretty isolating real fast."

"I can imagine." Bev said. *All the more reason to reach out to her own neighbors.* She finished her last sip of wine and sat back, full and happy. Raven was sitting in front of the fireplace, chewing intently on a toy that Colleen had bought for her. There was soft music playing on the stereo. She was so fortunate to have such good friends with whom she felt so relaxed. She knew she had made the right decision moving here. There was something about this place, this town, this environment, that felt right somehow.

She just hoped that nothing happened to change that.

*

Bev gathered up the small notecards she had made for her neighbors and stuffed them into the big pocket of her coat. She didn't know her neighbors' names yet, so she just addressed each one with the name "neighbor" and a smiley face. Her intention was to stick these inside each mailbox on her road since it was too awkward (and maybe dangerous?) to just walk up their long driveways to knock on their front door.

Her note was simple. *Hello, I just moved into the house with the red metal roof. I would love to meet you sometime, here's my phone number and email in case you ever need to get a hold of me.*

She didn't say much about where she was from or who she was or what she did for a living. It seemed a bit too friendly and maybe a bit presumptuous. Did her neighbors really care about this stuff? She didn't want to come off as some nosey parker who tells you a little bit too much in the hopes that you'll reciprocate.

The weather that morning was unsettled. Low clouds descended on the mountain peaks, obscuring them from view, and the skies were varying shades of gray to the west. It was supposed to snow later, maybe an inch or two. Bev made a mental note to try to fire up the ATV in case she would need to plow the driveway. She'd never used one before, but she had looked at an instruction video on YouTube and it looked fairly simple.

After too many weeks of no precipitation, she could finally smell moisture in the air ahead of the storm. She was looking forward to the cozy feeling of snow falling outside and a fire crackling inside, with cookies in the oven and some jazz playing on the stereo.

She decided to start at the end of the road with the notecards and work her way back home.

She walked past the first mailbox at the head of the drive-way where the dog disappeared the other day. There were stick-on reflective letters below the numbers on the black mailbox. *Lewiston.*

She walked all the way down toward the last mailbox and put the notecard inside. The road continued west, but became increasingly rough and narrow. Further down about a mile or more there were a couple of houses, but they were occupied only in the more temperate months when the road was passable, probably by people whose regular residence was in Texas or California or somewhere hot in the summers. She had driven down the road as far as she could one afternoon after she had put in an offer on her house in September, and had gotten about three miles down before encountering a gate and a "No Trespassing" sign.

The next mailbox was bigger and a dark green. It leaned a little bit to the left. She opened it up and saw it had a few days' worth of mail in it. She stuck her note on the top of the stack and continued down the road.

On the way back to her house, she looked up and was startled to see that there was a man at the *Lewiston* mailbox who hadn't been there when she walked past the first time. He was crouched down next to the post and rail fence that encircled the property. He was wearing a black knit cap and a plain brown coat. He seemed to be fixing the barbed wire that had sagged off the fence.

She held a notecard in her hand, unsure now whether she should just hand it to the man or put it into his mailbox right in front of him. He seemed very preoccupied by the task at hand, twisting the wire taught at the post with a pair of pliers.

She gauged how close she should get before saying hello. She didn't want to shout it. The man didn't seem to notice her. She could see that he had brought a toolbox and placed it next to himself. He must have walked from his house because there was no vehicle. From the side, she could see he had a bit of a five o'clock shadow and appeared to be middle-aged, if not older.

Close enough now, she cleared her throat. "Hello!" She kept her voice upbeat.

He didn't turn around. He didn't seem to respond at all. *Must not have heard me,* she thought, although that seemed unlikely. Strange. Maybe he was hard of hearing? It was also strange that he wasn't seeing her by now and acknowledging her. She was well within his peripheral vision.

She walked a little closer. There was a short embankment between them. "Hey neighbor!" She called again, a little louder.

He turned his head to the side quickly, as if startled, and leaned back a little as he turned slightly toward her without taking his hands off his task. "Oh. Hi." His voice was low and gravely, with a slight tone of irritation. He was straining to tighten the wire on the post. He turned back around toward his task.

Bev suddenly didn't know what to do. "I, uh—wanted to say hi and introduce myself."

"A-yup." He let out an exasperated breath and continued twisting the wire. Bev didn't know what to say next. Her cheeks flushed. The man reminded her of her father, gruff and dismissive. She turned and started walking back home, passing his mailbox on the left without pausing or even looking at it. She put the notecard she was holding in her hand into her pocket and left it there. She didn't want him to see what she was holding. Her shoulders rose up toward her ears and she quickened her pace. When she got to her driveway, she opened her mailbox and grabbed the letters that had been delivered the day before, slamming the flap shut afterward.

What was the guy's problem? Did he know she was the one who had bought the house? Maybe he thought she was just another out-of-state asshole, jacking up local property values and therefore, his property taxes. She'd heard from Connie that there were some people around town with misplaced resentment. They had bought their property when it was dirt cheap in the 80s or 90s and were now on a fixed income with a rising cost of living.

Thinking about this, she shook her head. If this was the case with this Lewiston guy, then he was making the wrong assumption. Property values were rising because the economy was improving. Home prices were rising everywhere. It wasn't her fault.

In any case, the encounter made her feel odd. As if she didn't belong here, even though this place felt more like home than anywhere else she had lived. Until now.

She stepped through the front door, threw her coat on the hook and kicked off her sneakers. She looked at the mail in her hand. A credit card bill and a letter from the attorney again. This day wasn't starting out well. She walked over to the kitchen and put the bill on the counter and the last notecard and the attorney's letter into the trash.

*

A few days later, Bev's remaining sense of comfort and optimism about her new home dissolved into dread.

That morning had started out so peaceful and upbeat. She woke up relieved to see that there wasn't any snow on the ground, as they predicted, since she hadn't figured out the ATV thing yet. The system had stayed tucked closer to the mountains, covering the jagged peaks in a blanket of white. She wanted to take a long walk with Raven to enjoy the views.

Neither of the two neighbors she left a notecard for had called or emailed her yet. She hadn't run into the Lewiston guy again, either. Trying to not let those two factors defeat her, she decided the best approach was no approach—simply go on with her life and let whatever happens, happen.

She and Raven turned left out of the driveway, heading east. No cars passed. She hadn't heard any warning barks or growls. Suddenly, out of her peripheral vision, just as Raven had stopped to sniff a rabbitbrush shrub, she saw quick movement between the trees across from where she was standing. The black dog, crouched and focused on Raven, rushed toward her silently. Instinctively, Bev yanked on Raven's leash and scooped her into her arms just as the black dog leapt up at them, teeth bared, snapping its jaws and growling.

She screamed as her entire body contracted. She felt the dog bounce off her as she spun around, putting her back to it, trying to shield Raven and herself from the attack. Raven began to squeal in response, squirming in her grip, trying to get free. She squeezed her as tight as she could, desperate to make sure she didn't get free.

She continued to scream, then yell, then curse wildly as the dog kept jumping on her, growling and sniping. Finally, it backed off and started to bark viciously. She kicked at the gravel road and managed to spray the dog with a few small rocks, which startled it momentarily, but long enough for Bev to begin running back toward her house with Raven still in her arms.

She had to stop a few times to turn around and rage at the dog some more to keep him from jumping on her. At one point, she had to kick the dog in the chest when it got too close, which had the effect of instantly quieting his bark as he re-assessed the situation. Instead of bolting, she backed up and managed to get halfway up her driveway before the dog began to approach again. Then she ran at full speed to the safety of her house, where she slammed the front door behind her, dropped Raven, and had to put an arm out against the wall to steady herself.

Raven stood in the kitchen, ears back and staring up at her, her eyes frantic.

Bev panted and her body shook. "Dammit! I knew that would happen! Of course!"

She went to the living room to look out the window to see if the black dog was still out there. It was. She saw it looking in the direction of the front door with a similar look to what Raven was sporting: ears back, tail tucked, posture stiff.

Back in the kitchen, she pulled out a broom from next to the refrigerator and went back to the front door. She opened it slightly at first, making sure the dog wasn't too close. As she swung it open, she saw the dog already retreating up the driveway toward the road. She gripped the broom handle in the same fist she shook in the air.

"Good riddance! Now stay the hell away!" She felt her rage boil over and for a second, considered going after the dog with the broom. But then she took another deep breath and went back inside.

As the morning went on, she had a hard time calming down. She wanted to call Colleen but knew she was probably busy with work and didn't want to bother her. She vented to the walls instead, and to Raven, who looked at her with curiosity.

"What's wrong with people? Why don't they fence their dogs so they're not out terrorizing the neighborhood? Or fence them *properly*?" She recalled her dog attack in the suburbs. "Dogs can kill people! That damned dog could have killed you!" Raven blinked and then opened her mouth wide in a tension-releasing yawn.

She recalled reading a news story about a woman who was mauled to death by a pack of dogs while out jogging in a rural area of eastern Colorado. Just random dogs that had not been fenced and had gotten together during the day while their owners were out ranching or working or whatever they did. Imagining what the woman must have experienced, Bev closed her eyes and shuddered. It seemed like such a horrifying way to die. It infuriated her that the owners of such dogs didn't seem to feel a sense of urgency about either restraining their dogs or wondering about where they were all day. It was inevitable that something like that would happen, and it was so avoidable.

Dogs were not the same in all situations. Just because they were friendly at home didn't mean they weren't capable of biting someone or even mauling a person or a small child. Didn't people worry about getting sued? Apparently not. Maybe people like that have never been sued so they had no idea what that was like.

Possibly, some people just didn't give a shit. They liked the idea that their dog patrolled their property and kept people from getting too close. They didn't give a shit that their dog wandered, marking its territory and crapping everywhere. Maybe they liked the idea of their dog being "footloose and fancy free". These were probably the same people who complained about the evils of big government and flew Don't Tread on Me flags on their pickup trucks. These were the same people who complained about people needing to take "personal responsibility" and not allow the "nanny state" to run their lives.

She knew the type. Strangely, her neighbor didn't seem the type. He didn't look like some gun-toting, beer-belly-hanging-out redneck. If anything, in her interaction with him he seemed *subdued*. Distracted. Like he couldn't be bothered.

If she had his number, she'd call him to let him know what happened. No, she'd probably *rage* at him. What the fuck? Your dog attacked me! But she didn't have his number. She didn't even know his first name.

She could go over there—later, in the evening after work hours —but by then it would be dark, and she wasn't about to go up that long driveway unannounced. It was risky. She didn't even know how far back his house was from the road. He might come out with his shotgun and an itchy trigger finger.

She could put a note in his mailbox. What would she write? How would she phrase it so that she wouldn't piss him off and start some kind of feud? She recalled Colleen's story of the Texas dude who was suing his neighbor. She thought of the way everyone was so damn defensive these days on social media. Whatever the situation, everyone had a comeback and an insult.

She wouldn't be surprised if he told her it was *her* fault for antagonizing his dog. That this wasn't the suburbs and maybe she shouldn't own such a scrawny, defenseless dog.

"This here's the mountains, lady," she imagined him saying. "You may want to keep that ridiculous dog in the house."

Ugh.

Would she be able to walk her dog here, *ever*? Or would she always have to worry about running into that beast? She imagined having to drive into town to walk Raven or keeping her dog contained in her yard. Neither option appealed to her at all. Here she had more space, lots of privacy, a larger property, less traffic and noise; and to have all that and feel *more* restricted? This wasn't what she signed up for. It's not what she imagined her life would be like here.

She was getting herself worked up and she knew it. The pattern was familiar. First, the anger, then the self-blame, then the despair. She didn't know how to snap herself out of it.

*

After putting away her supplies and cleaning up for the day, Bev decided to take another walk—alone, this time—to see if she would run into Lewiston. Perhaps she'd happen to be walking on the road as he returned home from work. She wasn't sure of his schedule, but if he worked typical hours, she might catch him. It would be dark in an hour, so she put her shoes and coat on quickly and stepped out her front door.

Still unsure of what she'd say, she was hoping she could at least get his attention and strike up a conversation. Introduce herself —or at least try. Ask him about his dog. Was it even his dog? She assumed it was, since she had seen it walk out of his driveway.

She turned left at the road, checked her mail, decided it was all junk and left it in the box for retrieving later. She looked in the direction of where the black dog had darted out of the woods this morning. There was no movement there now.

She walked all the way down the hill where she'd first seen the black dog and turned around. Of course! When she was hoping to see a car—his car or any car—she didn't. By the time she reached her mailbox again, the sun had just dipped below the trees to the west and cast a pink and golden glow on the sky.

A rustling sound behind her startled her and she spun around, her heart thumping in her chest.

The dog.

He'd walked up within ten feet behind her, his eyes inquisitive and his mouth open in a goofy dog grin.

"You've *got* to be kidding." She brought her hand up to her chest and steadied her breathing.

The dog's relaxed expression disarmed her.

"What do you want?" She demanded.

The dog glanced to the side, eyes squinted ever-so-slightly. She recognized the expression. Raven did the same thing when she was feeling stubborn and petulant, like when Bev wanted her to continue fetching a ball when she wanted something else, like a treat or a petting.

She went up to it slowly and carefully reached out to touch the top of its head. The dog sniffed her hand and stepped back.

"Come here. Let me see your collar," she said. Bev had an idea. Maybe the owner's number would be on it and she could at least call him and explain what happened. She approached the dog again, without hesitation this time. She hooked her finger under the worn leather collar and tugged. She rotated the collar and didn't see a tag.

She continued to hold onto the collar and the dog let her. She calculated her next move as the dog looked up at her, still panting. Why was he being so friendly now? A little Dr. Jeckyl & Mr. Hyde action?

Bev nudged the dog in the direction of his driveway. "Go home you mutt!" He looked back at her for a second and then sniffed the air, turned around and trotted in the direction of the scent, down the road.

This dog must have serious issues with other dogs. Maybe he'd been attacked before, too.

No matter. This dog was unpredictable. It was a problem. And in that moment, it felt exclusively like *her* problem.

*

The fire crackled in the wood stove as Bev sipped her tea, sat on the couch alongside Raven, whose ear she rubbed between her thumb and forefinger. She was starting to get sleepy, even though it was barely past 8 o'clock. The emotional havoc from earlier in the day was catching up with her.

Raven shifted her position, tucking her head farther down into her body and then letting out a long sigh. Bev was grateful that her quick response prevented the neighbor's dog from injuring Raven. At least not physically. Bev was certain that the incident further scarred Raven's psyche and would make her even more neurotic around dogs in the future.

She and Rick had adopted Raven as an 8-week-old puppy from a shelter in Denver. She was scrawny even then. The shelter staff thought she might have some Italian greyhound in her, mixed with some sort of terrier or a small black breed like a Schipperke. They had been looking for a compact dog, a companion for hikes and walks that didn't take up too much space in their house or cost a fortune to feed. Raven stood out from the collection of pit bull and lab mixes that composed most of the shelter's population. She was sleek, inky black, and had a long, skinny tail that arched down into a point of white fur at the tip. Her shiny black eyes were framed at the top with expressive eyebrows that easily communicated the basic dog emotions—fear, anticipation, pleasure or curiosity.

Bev enjoyed it when Raven watched her as she worked on creating her soaps and lotions during the day. It made her feel less lonely. Most of the time, however, Raven napped, happily content to spend the day languishing in a sunny spot on the rug or in her dog bed.

When Rick died, Raven kept Bev to a certain schedule of waking, feeding and walking that provided structure at a time when she felt ungrounded and directionless. Now, during this transition from city to rural life, Raven reminded her that as long as there were certain constants, like snuggles on the couch and long walks in nature, she would be okay.

Back in Denver, Bev managed possible problem dogs by crossing the street or hiking only in places where dogs were required to be leashed.

This was why this situation at this new house was troublesome. There really wasn't any other road to walk on, unless she drove to a different road. Even then, there was no place to park in order to go walking. She could drive into town, but that was a 15-mile drive and a half an hour away, one way. She didn't want to walk on her property because of prickly pear—a long-needled cactus that sprouted up everywhere and made it hazardous for Raven. Besides, even if she did clear some trails on her own property, unless she also fenced it, there'd be no guarantee the black dog wouldn't find his way to them.

This was something she never even considered before she moved here—that she wouldn't be able to walk her own dog without fear of being attacked. The idea that she wouldn't be able to walk her own dog at all in any sort of routine way was upsetting to her. She had as much of a right to enjoy the road as anyone else who lived here. Why did this neighbor of hers let his dog wander around as if he owned the entire neighborhood? As if the county road and everyone's yard was his yard, too? Bev certainly couldn't imagine letting Raven run around like that. It was rude. Not to mention that with all the wild predators living on the mesa, it seemed careless to allow a dog to free-range.

Wasn't her neighbor worried about his dog getting killed by a pack of coyotes?

Bev let that thought sink in as she took a long sip of tea. The dog could just disappear one day, and his owner wouldn't have a clue what happened. He'd probably assume it had gotten into trouble with a wild animal. This type of thing must happen frequently around here to pets that aren't fenced in. She seemed to recall her realtor making a comment about the mesa not being a great place for small dogs and outdoor cats, just for that very reason.

The fire was beginning to shrink, so Bev got up off the couch, poked the embers and added another log to the top. She got a whiff of the piñon smoke and closed her eyes to invite an old memory that emerged in that moment, of herself and Rick in Santa Fe around Christmas, walking back to their hotel after dinner in the Plaza. The golden light of the luminarias, the soft look of the stucco houses, and the smell of piñon wood smoke permeating the air. She closed the woodstove door and settled back next to Raven, who was curled up in the plaid couch blanket, sleeping.

What advice and insights would Rick have about this? He had a way of easing her mind, no matter what troubled her. He would probably tell her that she had every right to feel the way she was feeling, and that he would go over to the neighbor first thing in the morning to sort this out. She would trust that he would do so in a way that wouldn't piss off the neighbor, because he had a way of being incredibly diplomatic. No one could be angry at Rick.

Bev had no such talents. She'd pissed off plenty of people in her life. Her mother, her brothers, and most recently, one of her girlfriends back in Denver. Sometimes Bev kept her mouth shut just long enough to build up a lot of biting words behind her lips. It didn't take much to unleash them: a headache, a restless night, a delayed meal, a pain-in-the-ass customer.

She often wished she could stop wasting so much time being annoyed and angry and actually do something constructive or proactive. That's how Rick was. He wouldn't waste too much time complaining, he would just weigh his options, make a plan and take action. Boom. Just like that.

"A little less drama, Bev." He would say when she'd lay out her angst to him. She didn't like being shut down like that, because goddamn it, bitching about people often felt *so good.* Rick was not interested in gossip, a personality trait which fascinated Bev because it seemed so stoic and noble. He was able to stay focused on his tasks and his life without a desire to meddle in, or talk about, anyone else's life. He would often tell her that her penchant for drama didn't solve anything, all it did was agitate her. He was right.

Complaining about things to herself wouldn't solve any problems.

It wouldn't make the dog disappear.

Make the dog disappear.

An idea bloomed in her mind. A part of her wanted to keep the idea curled up tight, examine it for flaws, and put it away on a back shelf. Another part of her wanted to spring into action, give herself a high-five and laugh out loud.

It was an idea that seemed almost too simple, too obvious.

By the time she turned in for the night, she found herself hoping she'd run into the black dog again the next day. In fact, she looked forward to it with a fervor she hadn't felt in a long time.

*

The weather shifted overnight. Fast-moving, low clouds raced across the horizon and a cold wind rattled the house. Out her kitchen window, Bev could see curtains of what appeared to be rain or sleet obscuring the mountains to the east. Despite wanting to go looking for the dog before getting started on her day, Bev decided to wait out the weather and try venturing out around noon instead. It was Saturday and she didn't have any plans to go anywhere. She was all caught up on her soap inventory and orders, so there was no work to do. She spent the morning sipping coffee, scrolling through Facebook. She cooked fruit and pancakes for breakfast.

After doing her business in the small fenced area surrounding the back deck, Raven spent the morning curled up in her dog bed, guiltlessly napping.

Finally, around 12:30 pm, Bev unrolled her legs from underneath her, got up off the couch and put on her coat and shoes to go outside. Even though the wind had died down, the sky was a solid gray and the air was brisk and smelled of moisture. Whatever front was rolling in, it was bringing in the beginnings of winter.

She made a left turn out of her driveway and walked to the crest of the first rise in the road, which took about ten minutes. Once there, she scanned the gravel road and the surrounding woods. A squirrel fussed in the trees, squeaking incessantly as a warning either to her or to whatever was nearby. No other animals appeared.

She walked back up the road toward her house and halted as she neared her driveway. The Jeep Wrangler she had often seen driving down the road was now parked in front of her house. She approached it, unable to see if there was anyone inside due to the reflections on the windshield. As she got closer, the driver's side door opened and a woman got out and gave her a cursory wave.

"Hi Bev! I was just leaving you a note." Bev recognized her neighbor, the blonde woman she assumed to be in her early 30s. As she came around and extended her hand to shake Bev's, it surprised her that she appeared much older up close. Not in her 30s, but at least in her mid-40s, maybe even older. Her long blonde hair gave her a deceivingly younger appearance from behind the windshield driving past at 20 miles an hour.

"I'm Jess, your neighbor down the road," She smiled as she shook Bev's hand. "I got your note the other day."

"Oh yeah, of course," Bev smiled. "I was just out getting some fresh air."

"Yeah, it's getting cold, isn't it? Winter is just around the corner. I wanted to come by and say welcome to the neighborhood."

"Thanks, I am looking forward to meeting all the neighbors on this road," Bev said, then remembered her encounter with the man across the road the other day and thought, *well except that guy.*

"Where'd you move here from?" Jess asked.

"Westminster. A Denver suburb," Bev replied.

"Yeah, yeah, I used to live on the Front Range too. Arvada. My husband and I moved here ten years ago. You're gonna love it. It's an amazing place." Jess paused, looking up at Bev and smiling, as if waiting for her to agree. When Bev didn't say anything more, Jess cleared her throat and lifted her chin. "Oh! You know, I almost forgot why I came here!" She reached in and got something out of the car. "I have something for you."

She reached in across the driver's seat and pulled out a plastic-wrapped dinner plate, which she handed to Bev. "Here's some cookies I made. I hope you like them. They're oatmeal maple."

"That's sweet. Thanks."

"Sure, hope you like them." Jess said. She had dark, thick eyebrows that framed her soft and welcoming brown eyes. Her blonde hair hung straight back over her shoulders and Bev could see now from the roots that it was bleached, not natural. She wore a thick, denim coat that was partially zipped up over a faded plaid flannel shirt.

"Would you like to come in for some coffee or tea or something?" Bev asked. She made a mental scan of her house, wondering if it was tidy enough for visitors. She decided it was probably good enough, but Jess was already shaking her head.

"No, actually, I'm on my way to the grocery store. But I wanted to ask, would you like to come over for dinner next weekend? Are you available next Sunday, say 6 pm?"

The invitation was so casual and yet unexpected. In the many years she'd lived in Denver, none of her neighbors had invited her and Rick over for dinner. She imagined what it would be like, getting to know Jess, having friendly conversation over a glass of wine with the fireplace crackling. She was curious what her house was like, since she couldn't see it from the road.

"I would."

"That's great. I'm the second house on the right, the one with the big green mailbox. I live there with my husband Steve and a couple of German Shepherds, a cat, a horse and a couple of goats." Jess chuckled.

"That's a lot of pets." Bev said.

"Yeah, it can be a handful sometimes. But we love them all."

That certainly confirmed that the black dog wasn't theirs, but she had never seen any German Shepherds running around, either. They must keep them close to home. She had heard faint neighing and bleating before, though, and now she knew where those sounds were coming from. All the little mysteries of the neighborhood were being solved, one by one.

"Ok, well, we'll see you next Sunday, then." She handed Bev a piece of paper. "Here's the note I was going to leave on your door, inviting you to dinner. It has our number on it." Bev glanced at it without reading it and stuck it in her coat pocket.

Jess got back in the Wrangler and waved to Bev as she made a wide turn and drove off. Bev waved back. Once the Wrangler turned left out of the driveway, Bev lifted one side of the plastic wrap off the plate, brought a cookie to her mouth and bit off a chunk.

It was delicious.

*

Stuffing several slices of turkey into her coat pocket, Bev left the house right after finishing her second cup of coffee the next morning. Raven followed her as she went to the closet for her coat and sat down on the bench in the mudroom to put her sneakers on. Raven stared at her intensely, no doubt smelling the turkey and wondering why Bev wasn't reaching for the leash to take her along. Or why she wasn't offering her some of the meat.

"Sorry girl. I can't take you with me this morning. Soon, hopefully. And the treat isn't for you."

Raven backed up a step and let out an exasperated sigh—what Bev knew was dog for, "Fine, be that way."

Bev stepped out onto the driveway and flipped up the hood of her coat. It was still cloudy, and the temperature had dropped considerably overnight. There was a faint, sweet smell of piñon in the air from someone burning wood in a fireplace nearby. A mountain chickadee called out from the trees to her right, with its distinctive *cheeseburger cheeseburger—screeeeet* call.

She turned right out onto the road, opposite of her usual route but moving west, in the direction of Lewiston's driveway. There was a bank of much darker clouds on the horizon, which surprised her. Was it supposed to snow later? She forgot to check the forecast that morning. She wouldn't be surprised if it had gone from a forecast of party cloudy with a zero percent chance of precipitation to a blizzard warning overnight. This wasn't like in Denver, where there were many meteorologists with the best equipment to do accurate, long-term predictions. Here in south-west Colorado, you'd be lucky to know what kind of weather tomorrow would bring. Someone told her it was because of tricky aspects of the terrain, but she suspected it was because not enough people cared about accurate weather predictions for this part of the state.

She increased her stride, eager for things to unfold so she could see if her plan would actually work. She felt a shift in her attitude toward the dog, from a sense of dread about running into it to a sense of anticipation and curiosity. She wanted the dog to appear and approach her. Could the dog, wherever it was, sense this?

She heard that dogs can sense fear and will act aggressively toward you even if you think you're acting calm. She was afraid of the dog that ended up attacking her in Denver and always tried to walk past calmly. It hadn't helped. The dog *knew*.

But now that she had a plan, she wasn't pretending to be calm, she *felt* calm. A strange kind of calm. Almost as if she was asking —no, daring—the dog to try something.

If only the dog would show up. Where was he?

She approached Lewiston's driveway and put her hand in the pocket where she'd stuffed the slices of turkey. She hoped the moist, smelly meat would be as irresistible to the dog as she assumed it would. She took a deep breath and sighed. The wind picked and up whooshed through the trees. She heard a faint knocking or hammering coming from the direction of her house, but further east, maybe from one of the houses closer to the main county road, about a quarter of a mile away.

When she reached the driveway, she stopped. No sign of the dog or the man. She pondered her next move. Should she continue walking, hoping that spending more time on the road would lure the dog to her?

Should she try to go up the driveway in hopes that it would alert the dog and it would approach her?

Probably a bad idea if the man saw her. She didn't have a good excuse to be walking down his driveway, which was long and curved. Anyway, if he spotted her, it would certainly ruin her plan.

Maybe he was currently enjoying a leisurely breakfast and probably wasn't giving a second thought to where his dog was, or whether it was wandering around someone's property or getting into someone's business while that someone was trying to enjoy time outside or walking with their dog.

Asshole!

Why were people such assholes?

She was halfway back to her own driveway when she heard the rustling of gravel behind her. She jumped and let out a weak yelp when she realized the dog was behind her.

"There you are, you troublemaker."

Bev faced the dog squarely and pulled the wad of turkey slices out of her pocket. "Come here. I've got something for you. It's ok."

The dog stood perfectly still, looking right at her, its expression cautious. It sensed something, alright, and it wasn't Bev's fear, because she wasn't afraid. Bev extended her hand with the turkey and waved the slices in the air.

"Want this? Here doggo. Come get some meat." She raised her voice a pitch, trying to sound friendly and inviting.

They stood facing each other for what seemed like a minute, sizing each other up. Then he took a step toward her. And then another, head still help high, muscles tense and ready to bolt. Bev tore of a chunk of turkey and threw it on the ground between herself and the dog. The dog flinched but didn't retreat.

"That's right, come and get it you little fuckstick."

A few seconds later the dog carefully but deliberately approached the turkey slice. It sniffed it once and then gobbled it up greedily. It looked up at Bev, its demeanor slightly more friendly and open. But only slightly. She threw another slice on the ground, closer to her. The dog advanced on the meat and swallowed it up without tasting it.

She slowly started backing up, moving back toward her house. The dog followed, still keeping about 20 feet of space between them. She tore off another chunk of meat and threw it down. The dog's demeanor was relaxed enough now that she turned around and made her way up the driveway while still calling to the dog to follow her.

A few minutes later, she was standing next to her garage and the dog was closing the gap between them. She held out a piece of turkey as she squatted down, hoping to signal to the dog that she was friendly and had no ill intent.

With each chunk of turkey, the dog seemed to soften. It began to wag its tail ever so slightly.

Finally, the dog was close enough that Bev could offer it the last bit of turkey out of her hand.

She reached out to scratch his head while he licked and smacked his chops. He moved closer to her, sniffing her jacket for more turkey.

Grabbing him by the collar, Bev backed up slowly toward the side door of her garage. The dog hesitated and then braced his legs to resist the pull. She yanked a little harder and a second later he relented, letting her lead. With one swift move, she opened the door and pulled him into the dark garage, flipped on the light switch and shut the door behind them.

He looked up at her, then around the garage, and back up at her.

Bev's heart hammered in her chest. "That wasn't so hard. I guess you're friendlier than you seem without any other dogs around, eh?"

He cocked his head to the side as he looked at her.

She went over to a shelf on the other side of the empty bay where there were several tarps and furniture blankets stored from her move. She pulled the felt blanket off the shelf and placed it on the ground. "Here," she pointed, "Take a break. I'll be back with some food and water."

Ignoring her, the dog started sniffing the floor and exploring the two-car garage space. She figured she'd be able to leave without him fighting his way back outside—for the moment.

She left the light on for him as she went back to the house to find an extra dog bowl that she could fill with water and bring back to him.

*

She could hear him barking from inside the garage an hour later, as she walked from the house up the driveway with Raven, who kept pulling on her leash, wanting to investigate. She increased her pace and eventually by the time they reached the road, Raven had lost interest in the canine prisoner's protests.

At the road she stopped and listened. She couldn't hear the barking this far away, although she couldn't tell for sure. Was she imagining she was still hearing barking? The wind had picked up and the sound of it through the trees masked whatever barking there might be. What if the owner decided to go looking for his dog and the wind died down?

Well, no matter, she'd let the dog out before then, anyway. She just wanted an hour without having to worry about the dog running at them. Raven was happy to be out. She could tell because her head was high and she excitedly sniffed the air.

She walked in the direction of Lewiston's, passed it, and continued on to the end of the road to the gate. The day was still solidly cloudy and getting colder. In her rush to get out of the house she'd forgotten her gloves, and her hands were starting to feel stiff. She shoved them deep into the pockets of her coat, the right one still damp from the wad of turkey slices that were now in the stomach of the black dog.

As she neared her driveway, she heard a strange sound. Not a barking—this was more of a siren sound. Was that her fire alarm? No, that couldn't be. She had disabled those dreaded things in her house because they freaked Raven out when they started chirping arbitrarily in the middle of the night. Was it the wind whistling through a door? She put her head down and tilted her ear to the sound.

"What the hell? Is that *howling?*"

Oh no.

She hurried up and put Raven back in the house and then checked on the dog in the garage. She opened the door carefully so he wouldn't bolt out. He was standing in the middle of the empty bay. As if he'd been standing there ever since she locked him up inside.

"Shhhh! Stop it."

He barked at her.

"You're going to howl as soon as I leave, aren't you?"

He blinked once. Once for *yes.*

"If I let you out, you'll come back the next time I take Raven on a walk and attack her, won't you? And I bet you won't be fooled into following me next time, meat or no meat." Bev sighed and bit her lower lip. She had hoped the dog would just comply and wait quietly in the garage, but that wasn't going to happen. He'd keep barking, and howling, and maybe escalate to something like desperate scratching.

Bev felt annoyed and a bit angry at herself. She didn't expect this development. Isn't that always what happens? You have an idea and you think it's perfect until you learn that you can't control the outcome, can't control what people do, what animals do, or how nature behaves.

The good thing was that the dog seemed to wander around the neighborhood and the owner probably wouldn't miss him right away. She had time to figure out a Plan B.

What was Plan B?

God, she just wanted this dog GONE. Gone—as in, far away from here never to return. As in, no longer a problem. As in, she could walk her dog in peace and not be constantly looking over her shoulder or tensing up in anticipation of an attack.

The dog yawned and slowly lowered himself to the floor to lie down.

If she waited until after dark to do what she wanted to do, would his howling attract attention? She'd never seen anyone walking the road, so it's not likely anyone would hear him. Certainly they wouldn't be able to hear him from inside their vehicles.

What if the owner comes looking for him? And hears the howls as he approaches her front door to inquire about a missing dog? That would be bad. Very bad. How would she explain that? Maybe she could claim she found him wandering around her property and was going to call the animal shelter and kept him in the garage for safe keeping.

Maybe that would fly. Yes.

Bev brought the dog a bowl of food to go with his water and didn't go back into the garage until after dark.

*

No one came knocking on her door looking for a missing dog. In fact, the rest of the afternoon was uneventful. Bev cleaned the kitchen and made a couple of calls to friends back in Denver.

Bev hadn't thought about her "prisoner" in the garage much all day. Now she had to make a decision. If she left the dog in the garage overnight he'd probably soil the floor (if he hadn't already) and the problem wouldn't be any better the next day.

Was she really going to do it?

She got up and retrieved her purse from the closet. She left a couple of lights on in the house for Raven and so that she wouldn't be coming home to complete darkness. She locked the front door and made her way towards the garage.

Inside, she noted that the food bowl was still mostly full. He was lying on the floor instead of the blanket she set out for him. And he wasn't howling anymore.

She first opened the hatchback of her SUV and then went to retrieve the dog, who stood up and started backing away as she approached. She grabbed him by the collar and then picked him up—he was heavier than Raven but not much more so. His fur was long and silky but she could feel his rib bones protruding slightly. He didn't resist as she placed him in the back of the SUV and shut the hatch.

She opened the garage door by clicking the remote on her visor. The dog started to whine softly in protest from the back of the vehicle.

She backed up into the driveway without the aid of any lights. Because it was still cloudy, there were no stars or moon, and in the darkness she couldn't even see the outline of the trees lining her driveway.

She only passed one other car before she made her way to the main highway, which was several miles away. She noticed her hands were shaking a little bit and she had to think hard about which road to turn on to get to where she was going.

The dog had settled down now and was eerily quiet. She couldn't even see him when she looked in her rearview mirror. At the main intersection of town, she made a left and plugged in her phone so she could look at the map. Traffic was sparse. Nothing was open except the gas stations and grocery stores.

Several turns and twenty minutes later the paved road ended and she was driving on dirt again. She was far west on the Uncompahgre Plateau now. There were no houses in sight, no streetlights, no stop signs, and no traffic signals. There were several turnouts where a doubletrack disappeared into the piñons. After a short while, the landscape at the edge of her headlights turned from piñons into to taller ponderosa pines. An owl flew in front of her car and out of sight into the treetops. Then aspens flanked the road, then tall and gangly spruce and fir trees.

She slowed down at the next curve and her headlights illuminated a driveway with an open gate and a trash container. She guessed that meant there must be an occupied house at the end of the driveway.

This was as good as it was going to get. Not on a busy road. No one would see her. A house nearby. Perfect.

She pulled as far off the road as possible without crashing into the trees and turned off the engine and headlights. The night descended instantly, thrusting her into almost complete darkness and silence. The dog panted behind her.

She got out and felt her way to the back of the car, feeling wobbly because she couldn't even see the ground.

When she opened the hatchback the dome light lit up the car interior and the dog moved to jump out. She slammed the hatch closed and looked around.

The dog was gone.

Or else she couldn't see him. She waited a few moments for her eyes to adjust to the dark and scanned the woods for movement. It was no use. She couldn't see a thing in the featureless murk.

She held her breath so she could hear any movement. Nothing. Wherever he darted off to, he was quick and stealthy.

There was nothing to do except get back in the car and go home and hope the dog found its way to the nearby house. He was used to wandering around in the woods by himself all day, wasn't he? Maybe he was much more savvy than she imagined. She hoped so.

She got back in the car and as she made a slow u-turn, she followed the path of the headlights but they only penetrated a few feet into the trees. She didn't see him.

It would be okay now. It had to be. Did she miss anything? If she did, it was too late now. He was gone.

She turned on some music to distract herself and to make the hour-long drive home a little more bearable.

*

Sunny, clear weather once again settled over southwest Colorado. Bev was up before sunrise every day that following week, enjoying coffee, reading, and then walking Raven for an hour before getting started with her work.

On Sunday afternoon she got ready to go over to Jess's house for dinner. She picked out a loose and sexy black blouse to go over a pair of comfortable but clean jeans. She found herself actually looking forward to being social and meeting her neighbor. She had had a busy week with soap production, marketing, filling orders and driving to town to drop them off at the post office, but every evening she was restless. She looked into maybe joining a book club in town and pondered going to some of the shows at the Sherbino, a venue for music and theatre in Ridgway.

She decided against walking to Jess's house despite its proximity because she'd need a flashlight, and she suspected the one in the junk drawer had a weak battery.

As she pulled up Jess's driveway, she noticed all the lights were on in the house, even the porchlights. There were also four cars parked in the driveway. Was this a party? She had assumed she was the only one invited. Maybe this was her opportunity to meet more people.

She walked up to the front door and rang the bell.

Jess's husband Mark answered the door, introduced himself, took her coat and welcomed her into a large, open living room that looked incredibly warm and appealing, with wood-lined ceiling and a large hearth with a crackling fire. Two German Shepherds darted out toward her, tails wagging.

"Hi Bev. Don't worry, they're friendly," Jess assured as she got up from the couch to greet Bev.

The dogs sniffed for a few seconds and satisfied, turned back toward Jess, who gently commanded them to go lie down on their beds.

"Glad you could make it. You already met my husband, Mark. And this is Carol and Lee, some friends of ours who live down in town."

Bev smiled at the couple sitting on the couch next to Jess. Carol looked to be in her 60s with very short gray hair and a blotchy, red face. Lee was tall and lanky and looked down at his beer.

"Nice to meet you," said Bev.

"You too," Carol replied.

"And this is Ron, our neighbor across the street. Ron, this is Jess, our newest neighbor who bought the Watson house."

Lewiston!

He was clean shaven tonight, but she recognized his face. Her stomach dropped.

"Hi, welcome to the neighborhood, I'm Ron." he said as he clasped her hand firmly in his and shook it.

"Oh. Um, thanks. I think that we met. Or, I've seen you when I was out walking."

Ron's eyebrows furrowed. "Really? When was this?"

"The other day, I don't remember. I said hi. You were fixing your fence."

"Really?" Ron looked puzzled. His gaze lowered to the floor and then back up. "Oh wait. Yes, I remember seeing someone walk past. I didn't know who you were. Assumed you were a short-term renter over at Sal's house or something."

"Sal's house?" Bev asked.

"Yes, the last house on the right, before the unmaintained section. Sal is a part-timer who rents his place on AirBnB."

"Oh."

Now that she was looking at him up close, she saw that he was a bit older than she assumed. Maybe in his late 50s. He was handsome, with black hair graying at the temples and a nice smile. He was wearing a dark red, flannel, button-down shirt and dark denim jeans.

"Can I get you a glass of wine or a beer?" Jess asked as she touched Bev's elbow.

"I'll have a glass of red wine if you have it."

"Great! Make yourself at home." As Jess walked to the kitchen Bev sat down in a plush leather chair next to Ron. Her head was spinning. She wasn't expecting this to be a party and she certainly wasn't expecting to be introduced to the dog's owner.

Mark came back from where he had hung up her coat and sat down on the sofa perpendicular to the one Carol and Lee were inhabiting.

"So where are you from, Bev?" Matt asked.

"I moved here from the Denver area. I have friends that live in town. Colleen and Terry Landquist. Do you know them? No? Ok, well, I used to visit them here and I fell in love with this area. When my husband died I decided I wanted to move out of the city and live closer to my friends and the mountains."

"Are you retired?" asked Carol.

"No." Bev bristled. Why did everyone ask that question? "No, not retired. I own a business making and selling soap. Before that I used to work in marketing. Nothing exciting."

"Hey, I'd like to try some of your soap," Jess returned with a glass of wine that she handed to Bev. "Where do you sell them? Hit me up sometime."

"Ok, I will."

The conversation then turned to the weather ("It's going to snow overnight. Twelve to 18 inches they predict."), to the state of the gravel roads ("They've *got* to scrape soon, it's like a bombing range right now with all the potholes."), to livestock trivia ("One of our goats is pregnant, I think, but she hasn't gotten bigger."), to the local real estate market ("The bubble is going to burst soon.")

After polishing off the wine, Bev felt more relaxed and loose, and got up to pour herself a second glass and noticed that Ron followed her to the kitchen. He got himself a beer out of a big plastic tub of ice next to the counter where Bev was selecting an open bottle of wine.

"I heard you say that your husband died. My wife died six months ago. She had breast cancer. We had been married for eighteen years."

Bev turned her head to look at him and their eyes met. "I'm sorry to hear that. It's tough, isn't it?"

"Yes, it is. I miss her every day."

"I know. It can feel pretty lonely. I'm glad I at least have my dog, Raven, to keep me company."

"What kind of dog is Raven?"

"She's a mix between something like a greyhound and a black lab but a little bit smaller." Bev smiled at Ron, who nodded as if agreeing with her assessment.

"I have a dog, too. His name is Bones. He's been missing about a week."

"Oh no." Bev's stomach lurched again. She took a big gulp of the wine.

"Yeah, I can relate to what you're saying about your dog keeping you company. That's why I adopted mine. He's gotten me through some rough patches, ya know?" Bev noticed he had an intensity to his eyes. She looked away.

"I called him Bones because he was pretty skinny when I got him. He's a sweet dog but I had trouble keeping him fenced in. Probably a ranch dog that didn't make the cut and was given up. Probably not used to fences and houses. Anyway, he gets out a lot, but he always come back. Until last weekend when he didn't."

Shit, shit, shit.

Bev assumed he was an owner that didn't give two flips about where his dog was and what he was doing. Her head swam in conflicting thoughts and feelings.

"I'm sorry," she said. "Maybe he wandered off and someone found him?" She was trying to sound consoling. "Maybe he's okay?"

"Have you seen him?"

"Me?"

"Yeah, he's a border collie mix. Black dog. Longer fur?"

"No." Bev's cheeks burned. "No, I don't think so. Maybe?"

Did Ron know something? His tone was odd. Like he was testing her rather than inquiring. Or was it her imagination? Maybe she should have admitted seeing the dog on her walks. She took a handful of peanuts out of the bowl Jess had set out next to the drinks and popped them into her mouth.

"Maybe you're right," Ron said. "Maybe someone picked him up. If that's the case, I hope they take him to a vet or the shelter, so they'll scan his microchip. The other possibility is wildlife and I just don't want to think about that."

Bev's heart pounded in her chest. He's microchipped? Oh, no. No, no, no!

That means that if Bones finds his way to the right person, Ron will get a call. And what will he think when he discovers his dog ended up 40 miles away?

Maybe she can track him down. It's not too late, is it? Maybe he's still around. Yes, it's been five days. There's a chance, isn't there? First thing in the morning, that's what she'll do. She'll go up there and hike around, bring some treats. If he made his way to someone's house it sounds as if he won't stick around long before he escapes again. She'll find him and he'll be hungry and be easy to lure back to the car with treats. Yes. And then she'll bring him back, release him. Like nothing happened. Like he just went on an adventure and decided to come home.

Like he wasn't kidnapped and dumped by some psycho.

She could barely taste the peanuts she'd been chewing. Suddenly she just wanted this shindig to be over with. Her face felt numb.

Ron reached into his pocket for his cellphone. "Hey, let me give you my number so you can text me if you see him, ok?"

If this had been under any other circumstance, Bev would have felt a pang of excitement that this handsome man was asking her for her number. But she felt zero flirtatious energy from him. He looked at her expectantly, his fingers poised on the screen of his iPhone. She gave him the number and he sent her the text, which she wouldn't see until she got back in her car where she left her phone.

During dinner, conversation remained on "safe" topics—work, living in the country, hiking trails, home projects. Distracted and uneasy, she didn't say much unless someone asked her a direct question.

The evening wrapped up a couple of hours later and Bev ended up sharing her contact information with Carol, who asked her about going on a hike sometime. Jess and Matt mentioned a musical performance they wanted to attend later in the week and asked if she was interested in joining them. Ron left before she did, but not before telling her to call or text if she saw his dog.

By the time she finally pulled into her garage that night, the wind picked up and it started snowing.

*

She was dreaming of a blizzard and searching for Bones when she was startled awake by Raven whimpering next to the bed. She reached down and caressed her dog's head to reassure her.

"Hey, hey. You're ok. What's going on? Do you need to go out?"

She picked up her phone that was charging on her nightstand and looked at the time. 3:10 am. She got up and followed Raven downstairs and to the back door. She turned on the porchlight and saw that the snow had already accumulated at least six inches. The wind was still whipping the flakes around and a drift had formed against the door.

Raven stuck her snout up against the doorframe, groaning impatiently.

"Geez, do you have tummy troubles or something?" she asked as she opened the door and watched Raven dart out and cut a path through the snow and out to where she disappeared in the darkness to do her business. She shut the door and shivered. It was highly unusual for Raven to want to be let out in the middle of the night. She hadn't fed her anything unusual and there was little chance she could have eaten anything that upset her stomach. Weird.

Her thoughts drifted to Bones. Hopefully he was inside somewhere and not out in this mess. Tendrils of her nightmare surfaced and re-submerged. The whimpering she heard in her dream must have been Raven wanting to be let out.

She scrapped her idea of driving up to the plateau this morning to look for him. She wasn't going to risk driving up there after this storm. She doubted the county plowed that far up.

Bev ran through the scenarios in her mind. Getting stuck on the road. Getting lost in the snowy woods and no one knowing where she was. Finding the dog dead. Meanwhile, Raven still hadn't returned to the door. She either had diarrhea or something else was going on. Did she sense something outside? An animal? Is that why she wanted to go out? She waited a few more minutes and contemplated having to get dressed to go look for her. She didn't want to do that, but she worried that Raven may have found something outside or gotten cornered by a coyote out there—or worse.

She was just about to go back upstairs to get dressed when she saw movement at the window next to the door. Raven! Covered in snow, desperate to return to the warmth of the house.

"What's going on with you?" she asked as she let her back in. Not waiting for an answer, she went back to bed.

She rolled from one side to the other, trying to get comfortable and sleepy. Wind gusts sprayed snow against the windows. This was her first snowstorm in her new house, but she'd seen winters here when she visited in the past. This early in the season the snow might be gone in a day or two because the days were still above freezing.

Normally, she would have welcomed the first snow and looked forward to doing some snow shoeing or skiing. But tonight, a dull dread settled over her.

She fucked up. She should have made it a point to talk to Ron about his dog before she did what she did. But he seemed so cranky the day she walked past, and Bev assumed he'd be dismissive—or worse.

It's too late now, she thought as she rolled over onto her back. If she called Ron to tell him what happened and what she did and why, he'd be so pissed. He'd probably have her cited for animal cruelty or something. Jess and Mark would probably find out from Ron about what she did and she'd be labeled a lunatic and they wouldn't speak to her again, let alone invite her to anything.

She had originally hoped Bones would find his way to a welcoming and dog-friendly home, that he'd be okay and her shameful secret would never be revealed.

But now she hoped he wouldn't find his way to any human. At least, no one who would do the responsible thing and get him scanned for a microchip. Maybe he'd find some campers up there and they would take him home, preferably somewhere far away, like Texas or California.

That seemed far-fetched to Bev, but she still entertained the idea.

Barring that, she hoped his demise would be short and relatively painless. Maybe hypothermia. Maybe tonight. She groaned. Damn it.

What was it, exactly, that she thought she was sparing herself by capturing Bones and dumping him on the plateau? She felt she couldn't confront Ron, sure, that was one reason. But why not bring an air horn or pepper spray on her walks with Raven to discourage Bones from approaching?

She didn't know. The moment she heard the dog barking and howling from inside her garage, threatening to expose her, something shifted in her mind. A rage welled up inside of her, and the thought that this dog was going to ruin this dream she'd had of living in the mountains close to Colleen and Terry, of finding peace and contentment after years of grief and longing and searching—it made her a little...

Crazy.

It made her crazy. Yes.

She had wanted this life for so long, even before Rick got sick and died. She never quite fit into city life. It was noisy, smelly and dangerous. The dog had threatened her vision of starting fresh and being happy. The thoughts and feelings about the wandering dog were too much like how she felt after the dog attack in Denver: fearful and contracted.

The dog had become ridiculously powerful in her mind.

She just wanted it gone.

She hadn't thought it through.

She had wanted complete control over a situation that was now (and probably always was) out of her control.

*

Another inch fell overnight, and at dawn the skies were clear. Bev's thoughts were clearer too, and she decided to drive up to look for the dog after all.

She texted Jess to thank her for a lovely dinner and to promise that she'll invite her and Mark for dinner soon. Jess texted her back right away, telling her they looked forward to it, and did she ski? They made tentative plans to go up to Telluride in January when conditions were good.

If her search for Bones came up empty, maybe next week she might text Ron to ask if his dog had returned. That seemed like something a good neighbor would do. And anyway, he intrigued her. She wanted to talk to him again.

After getting some tasks out of the way, Bev packed some lunch meat, put on a parka and snow boots, and left the house around 11 o'clock to make the drive back to where she had left Bones. She hoped she could park the car up the road from there and then wander around the woods to look for his tracks.

She barely made it to the crest in the road in front of her property when she saw a truck approaching. She slowed down and got all the way over to the right. As the truck got closer, she recognized it was Ron's. There was a black shape sitting next to him on the passenger seat.

A dog. Bones!

She braked and watched as Ron slowed way down and then lowered his side window.

They made eye contact. Bones started barking at her from his side of the cab, then walked over Ron's lap and almost jumped out of the truck before Ron pulled him back in and rolled his window back up.

She was still processing what was happening when she saw Ron turn his head back to the road without so much as a smile, wave or acknowledgement.

As he drove past, he accelerated again. She lifted her hand in greeting almost as an afterthought, a reflexive gesture. He was already gone and she didn't think he'd noticed.

She kept her foot on the brake for a few seconds, contemplating what to do next.

The drive up to the plateau was pointless, obviously.

She turned her SUV around and drove slowly back up to her house. There was a heaviness in her core that she hadn't felt in a long time.

Back in her kitchen a few minutes later, she picked up her phone and navigated to her recent calls. She scrolled down and touched on the entry she wanted. The phone rang three times before Colleen picked up.

"Hey Bev, what's up?"

"Are you busy? I need to talk to you about something."

"Of course! What's going on? You sound upset."

"Yeah, I am. Something happened. And I need your advice."

Bev put on the tea kettle and sat down at the counter, her head in one hand, phone in the other, elbows on the cold granite slab. She really didn't want to have this conversation, but the alternative was an inky cavern with no exit.

She took a deep breath and began to tell her best friend her side of the story.

GIG

"One day, in retrospect, the years of struggle will strike you as the most beautiful." – Sigmund Freud

The Craigslist ad read:

Wanted: A rugged, fit individual with high clearance 4WD vehicle, and experience reading topographic maps to set up a trail camera and hike up to it once a week. The location is approximately an hour drive east of Ridgway/Ouray but another 2-hour hike or so from where you'll park. Duration of gig is starting immediately and lasting possibly through the end of September. You'll be compensated well. Serious inquiries only.

Kylar noticed the ad in the "Jobs" section under the subcategory, "Gigs". She had just posted a couple pieces of climbing gear in the "For Sale by Owner" section of the app and then switched to browsing the jobs. Usually, there weren't many noteworthy posts in that section, but every once in a while, she'd find one-off gigs where she could make extra cash, such as when she helped bartend at a wedding in Telluride, or when she guided a private ski mountaineering trip south of Ouray for a couple visiting from Chicago.

This particular ad had just been posted the day prior and the description intrigued her.

She'd never seen a gig quite like this one, where a person was willing to pay for someone to essentially go for a hike once a week. Her immediate thought was that a hunter wanted to track game, but it was late May and hunting season for large game didn't start until fall. It may be something to do with the forest service, but they usually have plenty of unpaid volunteers for things like monitoring various aspects of wilderness.

Could it be a private company that was doing its own monitoring?

An hour drive east of Ridgway could be the Owl Creek Pass area, or the Uncompahgre

Wilderness, she thought. The ad also said it was a two-hour hike one way, which could mean anything from twelve miles roundtrip for a "rugged and fit individual" or six miles roundtrip for the average person.

Neither were a problem for Kylar. She was an alpinist who'd summited the tallest peak in the continental United States (Mount Whitney), scaled Denali in Alaska, and did extensive backpacking and mountaineering in British Columbia. Doing a twelve-mile hike in the San Juan mountains didn't worry her. She also drove a lifted Chevy pickup truck, so the all-wheel-drive, high-clearance vehicle requirement wasn't an issue, either.

Sweet, Kylar thought. She hit the "CONTACT" button and wrote a response.

Hi, I saw your ad and I would like to learn more about this. I'm an experienced hiker and mountain climber and own a vehicle that can handle just about anything. I'm available to speak on the phone today after 5 p.m. or you can email me back.

As much as her interest was piqued, she wasn't going to hold her breath while she waited to hear back. People who posted or responded to Craigslist ads weren't exactly reliable. When she posted ads, she always made sure to respond to every single person who inquired, and she wasn't one of the flakey "no shows" when purchasing something herself. But there was something almost too good to be true about this ad. Maybe it was the person's idea of "well compensated".

Still, even if it didn't pay much or wasn't a good fit, she was curious to learn who posted the ad and why.

With that thought, she swiped up and exited the app. She couldn't linger too long online because was late meeting her friend Sage. They were going to drive down to Durango together and do some climbing.

It was a very warm day, already in the 60s before 7 a.m. and forecast to get up into the 80s later that afternoon. There were small, fluffy clouds building above the mountains that usually didn't amount to anything this time of year. Kylar plugged in her phone and selected a playlist, eager to spend the day outside. If things worked out, she might also have a new, interesting gig this summer that didn't involve a kitchen or a mop bucket.

*

The call came in the following morning. Kylar saw the local area code and picked up after two rings.

"This is Kylar."

"You responded to my Craigslist ad and I'm calling you with some more information."

The voice was male, slightly raspy, possibly an older person. Sensing the ball was in her court, she hesitated, not sure if she should just ask the most obvious question or start to talk about her qualifications first. To his credit, the man didn't try to fill the few seconds of silence with more words. He simply waited.

"Right, thanks for calling," Kylar said. "Yes, can you tell me some more about this job? Who's it for? What are the exact tasks you require?"

"The job is for a project I'm doing. The exact tasks are that you'll set up a trail camera in a tree in an approximate location between Mount Baldy and Courthouse Mountain but north of the Wetterhorn Basin. And then go back each week to download any images the camera took to your phone, then email or text them to me the same day you go up there, if possible. I need this done once weekly. Doesn't need to be the same day each week, but it makes sense that it's spaced a few days apart. I can show you on a map where I need you to place the camera. It's about two miles from the Cow Creek trail. Are you familiar with the area?"

Kylar brought up a mental image of the area the man described. There were two roads in and out of there where the creek flowed. One was County Road 8 and Owl Creek Pass, a gravel road that went up and over the Cimarron Ridge from Ridgway to the eastern side of the Uncompahgre Wilderness, and County Road 12, which crossed the creek and became a rougher road that dead-ended. From what Kylar remembered from her explorations, the area he was referring to was a wooded canyon between two mountain ridges that ran north and south. She'd hiked one of the popular trails there to access the top of Courthouse Mountain, a square-topped slab towering more than 12,000 feet above two evergreen basins. She had a good sense of the terrain. It was steep and over-grown with a mix of aspens, 100-foot tall Douglas fir trees, spruce trees, and gambel oaks. There were no structures, no paved roads, and no cellphone service back there.

What did this old man want to do in that kind of remote area?

"Yes," she said. "I know the area. I mean, I haven't been exactly where you're describing, but I've hiked both Courthouse and Baldy."

She heard the old man let out a single, satisfied grunt. "Excellent."

"I'm sorry, what was your name?" Kylar asked.

"My name is Tom. Tom McDougal. And you are Tyler?"

"No, KY-LAR, with a K," Kylar said, enunciating each word and speaking slightly louder.

"KY-lar. Ok, Kylar, what I'm interested in is hiring someone who can read a map, handle a long hike, and who won't flake out on this responsibility after doing it once. Is that you?"

This guy is a little crotchety, thought Kylar. *Already has an attitude. Maybe he's used to disappointment.*

"That could be me," Kylar replied, her tone slightly amused. "I'm certainly qualified to do this work for you. I have the physical ability and a sturdy truck. I also have the discipline and time to follow through on the project." Kylar realized she was in job interview mode, making it all about what *he* wanted and not about what *she* wanted. She'd made that mistake before. So she suddenly switched gears. "Whether or not I *will* do it just depends."

"On what?"

"On what the pay is." *Duh.*

"Well, young lady—if you're as good as you say you are, and that's yet to be determined, then I'm prepared to pay you $250 for each time you complete the task."

Two hundred and fifty dollars?

Kylar's jaw nearly dropped to the floor. This guy was going to pay a thousand dollars a month for someone to do some hiking? Who was this guy, some kook? Kylar couldn't help but stifle a laugh. Then she composed herself, straightened her shoulders and cleared her throat.

"If that's the case," Kylar said, "then I'm in. What's the next step?"

"You'll have to come over to my house and get the camera and the instructions. How's tomorrow at 9 a.m. sound? I'll text you my address."

*

Kylar worried that she'd end up at some sketchy trailer park on the outskirts of town, facing a wild-eyed, long-haired geezer with an ax to grind (maybe literally), but when she pulled into Tom's driveway five minutes before their appointment, she breathed a sigh of relief.

He lived in a ranch-style home in the larger town of Montrose, a half an hour's drive from her apartment in Ridgway. The lawn in front of his house was verdant and meticulously groomed. Two tall, mature elm trees created a welcoming tunnel of shade from the road all the way to the front door. A freshly planted pot of petunias decorated one of the two steps leading up to the porch.

He answered the door almost immediately and invited her inside. He was of average height, balding with gray, closely cropped hair, and had a slight paunch pushing against his t-shirt. He wore wire-rimmed glasses that made him look like a retired accountant. He led her to the back of the house to a bright kitchen with white cabinets and blue countertops.

"Have a seat here," he pointed to the nook off the kitchen, to a round table with four chairs in front of a window, "and we'll go over everything."

On the table was a trail camera and a topographic map, opened and laid flat, with a highlighter, a pen and a pad of sticky notes on top. Kylar pulled out one of the chairs and sat down opposite Tom, who got his iPhone out of his pant pocket and placed it on top of the map.

"You have your phone?" He asked, then nodded as Kylar placed hers on the table. "You'll want to download this app that goes with the trail camera." He showed her his phone screen and she made note of which one, downloaded it, and waited for Tom.

He showed her how to turn the camera on and off, where the battery compartment was and how to open it, and how to set it up using the phone app.

"You'll want to set the sensitivity to something in the medium range here," he pointed, "because I don't want to be taking a thousand photos of birds or whatever. It's also important that you set the camera up about five feet off the ground, around a tree without branches in the line of sight, because every movement will trip the camera, and if it's windy it'll take too many photos of the swaying branches."

"Makes sense," said Kylar, trying to sound agreeable.

He then showed her how to connect her phone to the camera and upload the images, then how to clear the cache from the camera.

"You may need to move it to somewhere else in the general area or take it to another area altogether. I'll let you know," said Tom.

"Got it. What are you taking photos of? Big game? Since you want it five feet off the ground," Kylar asked.

"I definitely don't want to be taking photos of squirrels," Tom replied, but didn't elaborate further.

Jesus Christ, really?

"Yes," she agreed, "But, what's this for? I mean, hunting season isn't until September, right?"

"It's not for hunting," Tom answered, his tone slightly abrasive, then looked at her for a second longer before adding, "This is a personal research project. It has nothing to do with tracking game for hunting."

"Ok." She got the feeling that if she pressed him further, he'd ask her to leave, so she nodded and looked down at the map. He had circled an area with the yellow highlighter. The circled area depicted the Cimarron Range, a north-south range of spired peaks adjacent to another range that was part of the northern San Juan Mountain. A long, thin, blue line dissected two steep ridges to the west: Cow Creek. A black dot was drawn and shaded in with marker, somewhere west of the peaks but east of the creek.

"This here is the general area where I'd like you to place the camera. It's about two miles south of the trailhead, along this ridge right here," he pointed. "You'll need to park your vehicle somewhere here, and then follow the trail until you get to this bend here." He touched the map with his index finger lightly. "Then go straight south. I don't know what this area looks like right now. It's been many years since I've been up there. Could be some serious overgrowth or downed timber there, I don't know. But you said you can handle a difficult hike."

"Yes, it's not a problem. I traverse that kind of terrain all the time when I go climbing."

"Mountain climbing?" Tom asked.

"Yep. That's what I do. Mountain climbing, rock climbing, alpine expeditions."

"Huh," Tom rubbed his chin and raised his eyebrows. "Where have you climbed?"

"The Canadian Rockies, the Cascades, Cerro Fitz Roy in Argentina, and last year I was part of an expedition in Nepal to summit Annapurna," Kylar said. "But we got turned around due to weather. I hope to get back there someday, though."

"Impressive," Tom said sincerely. "When I was your age, I wasn't a climber, but I did do a lot of backpacking and trail running. I lived in Ouray for 20 years and explored so many places. Unfortunately, I can't do that anymore. Weak heart. Doctor told me I had to move to lower elevations and avoid high altitude and physical exertions. So here I am."

"I'm sorry to hear that."

"Eh. Don't be," Tom waved her apology away. "I've done enough of that stuff in my life. In my twenties, right after college, my wife and I bought some acreage in Alaska—near the town of Wasilla if you know where that is, and I built a cabin on our property. Did a lot of fishing and hunting, and lived off of that and a garden, since the closest grocery store was forty miles away. We raised our kids there before moving to Colorado."

"That sounds idyllic. Why did you move?" Kylar looked past Tom to the living room, where she noticed several framed family photos on the mantle above the gas fireplace.

"My wife wanted to live closer to her parents. By then the kids were teens and it was better for them to be in a school around kids their age. I got a job with a local outfitter, and then worked for the county." He paused, thought for a second, and added, "It worked out."

Tom slid the map off the table and began folding it up. Kylar took that as a signal that the meeting was over. She pushed back her chair and picked up the camera.

"I'm just curious," she said, "about how much you're paying. You said two hundred and fifty each week, for each retrieval of the photos. That's a lot of money to pay someone to do this. Is there a catch?"

Tom chortled. "No catch. I'm paying that much because that's the only way I could get anyone to do this week after week. Don't you think?"

That's not what I'm asking, thought Kylar.

"Agreed. But this...er...project of yours. It must be something important? Because that's quite the expense to be paying someone to retrieve nature shots. Or whatever."

"Some things are more important than money, Kylar. Much more important." Tom said bluntly and stood up.

She didn't have anything to say in that moment. She stood up too and followed him to the front door, which he had opened for her. Before she walked back down the driveway, they briefly discussed her schedule and when she anticipated setting up the camera, then they shook hands.

Kylar pulled out of Tom's driveway, still pondering what Tom said at the kitchen table.

Some things are more important than money, Kylar.

Yes, she thought, *some things were more important than money.* That's why she chose the kind of life she had for herself: moving to where her heart called her, working odd jobs, not owning much of any value other than her truck and her climbing gear. She only had enough money in her bank account to buy food, gas and pay rent for a few months. She didn't have a retirement portfolio and didn't own real estate or stocks. She didn't even have health insurance, which she knew was not very prudent given her activities, but she was okay with that risk for the time being. *If I get into debt because of a broken leg or arm, oh well,* she concluded.

It was never about money for her.

For her, it was about being close to the mountains, about experiencing life on her terms, doing what she loved, and being free. When she was on a mountain and laser-focused on her next move, completely mindful of where her limbs were in relationship to the rock wall, she wasn't worrying about whether she'd be able to pay her rent. Her life literally hung in the balance between her fingers, toes and tools. To her, that was freedom. It was freedom from overanalyzing and ruminating. It was freedom from having to follow a script or adhere to someone else's expectations. High on the mountain, thousands of feet above flat ground, she was entwined with the forces surrounding her: the wind, the granite, gravity, and the warmth of the sun on her back.

Tom's "personal project" must be that "more important than money" thing. But what? What was he trying to accomplish with the trail camera? It was understandable that he would be reticent to be transparent with his intentions and plans. He didn't know her, and she hadn't done anything to prove herself yet, besides show up for their first meeting on time.

She'd figure it out eventually. She intuited from his demeanor that she had to be patient. Meanwhile, though, she congratulated herself for finding and landing this intriguing assignment; one that meant she'd be forced to discover an area she'd hadn't yet explored. And that was always a good thing.

*

The next day, she was up before sunrise to set up the camera. She estimated the amount of time it might take her to drive to the trailhead and do the roundtrip hike. Hopefully, she'd be back before noon and would still have time to do some rock climbing in Ouray that afternoon.

She headed east out of Ridgway and turned onto County Road 12, an improved dirt road that flanked a series of small moraines and hills and took her beyond the pastures and ranches of the valley floor. The road dipped down to cross Cow Creek, turned into a rough four-wheel-drive road, crossed the creek again a mile later, before it dead-ended at the trailhead. She wasn't sure how the crossing would go; creeks typically ran high with snowmelt this late in spring. Tom hadn't given her any clues about what to expect and she didn't have any personal experience with Cow Creek. Her truck was capable of crossing high water as long as it wasn't flowing too fast and high, so she tried to remain optimistic.

She descended the last hill before the creek and decided she'd have no trouble driving across the short stretch to the other side. She rolled forward over the creek bed and heard water slosh under her truck as she drove over basketball- and grapefruit-sized rocks. She negotiated deep channels that had been formed by rushing water in previous summers.

As much as she appreciated the relatively uneventful drive across, the low flow concerned her. Normally this time of year, rivers and creeks downslope of the mountains would be raging.

It had been a dismal year for snowpack. Almost everyone in town lamented that there'd be watering restrictions that summer. She'd spoken to a couple of ranchers who wondered if they'd be forced to sell their cattle if they didn't get enough water for their pastures. Drought was the perennial worry in this part of the country and the urgency to figure out how to stretch unpredictable and increasingly scarce water resources was intensifying each year.

She accelerated out of the creek and back onto the road, avoiding ruts and rocks. There was no one else on the road, which was a good thing, since the road had narrowed substantially after it crossed the creek. Her truck occasionally brushed against thick stands of gambel oak. She passed a dozen cows at one point and had to veer to avoid hitting a couple that were grazing close to the road. Ranchers must have moved their herd into the national forest to graze earlier than usual. After another mile, the road passed through small stands of aspen and ponderosa, and she passed a Forest Service sign for Courthouse Trailhead. She'd hiked that trail from the other side to summit the flat top of Courthouse Mountain. She didn't even know the trail kept going, and ended up on this side of the mountain.

She continued on, the vegetation changing from ponderosa to lodgepole pine and spruce. Out of the trees, she was once again at the creek, this time on the other side and parallel to it. She crossed to the other side and back again before rejoining the road on the east side. In the near distance she saw a steep, narrow valley between two mountains. The mountain farthest south was still covered in snow down to what she estimated to be about 10,000 feet. The mountain closer in just had thin patches at the top.

The road ended in a small parking area close to the creek, with several fallen logs blocking further motorized travel. She'd passed a trailhead sign for Cow Creek, so she knew she was in the right place. Now she had to continue another two miles or so up the trail and then venture off where Tom had indicated on the topographic map, which she had included in her daypack along with the camera, her cellphone, some snacks and a quart-sized water bottle.

After the first relatively flat stretch, the hiking trail became increasingly steep. She estimated that she was gaining altitude at a rate of about five hundred feet every half hour. She reached a series of switchbacks and put her head down, leaning her body into the incline, her gait nimble and her breathing rate elevated but steady.

She was slowed down considerably mid-way up the switchbacks by jackstraw—fallen trees that crisscrossed over the trail. She had to climb over or under logs that ranged from two to three feet in diameter, with branches that stuck out and snagged her clothing and scratched her arms. Then there were thin, crooked twigs that nearly poked her in the eye. Judging from the bare limbs and rotting bark, the trees had blown over some time ago, perhaps in a windstorm after a particularly wet spell during which the ground had soaked and softened.

She had to keep referring to her GPS phone map to make sure she was still close to the trail. The trail up to the jackstraw was faint anyway, but the debris completely buried it.

Finally, she was out of the jackstraw and on more level ground but on a sloped ledge. She looked up at the massive wall to her right that towered over the treed valley below. She stopped to drink some water and got out the map and her phone to see how much further she needed to go. On the map, the trail ahead zigzagged up another set of switchbacks, and it was right before that that she needed to set up the camera. There was a small creek on the map that didn't quite cross the trail at that point but led into a shallower drainage than the one she'd been traversing.

She arrived at the first switchback and set down her daypack to retrieve the camera. She looked around. She was surrounded by miles of wilderness extending into a green, tree-blanketed canyon heading southeast on one side, with craggy rock outcroppings and snow-covered peaks in the distance. It was breathtaking. She was completely alone here, not having encountered any other vehicles on the road up and not having seen any other hikers. Based on the condition of the trail, she wouldn't have expected to run into too many hikers anyway. According to the map, the trail she was on dead-ended at a basin at least eight miles further, so the chances of running into anyone on this hike were near zero in her mind.

She looked up the slope to her left, examining the trees to determine which one to select to mount the camera. Most of the trees had branches that were too low to the ground and would obscure the field of vision. Then she spotted what looked like a very tall and old Douglas fir. The lowest branch was above her head and the tree itself faced the trail but was set back enough from the trail to include a wider field of vision. *Perfect.*

She mounted the camera with a long, brown strap that Tom had given her and checked the resulting image on her phone to make sure it covered the trail at the right height. Then she initiated the settings that Tom had wanted and stepped back, checking the placement. She waved at the camera, knowing it would take her photo. The camera was well camouflaged in the shadow of the tree and surrounded with brown and green vegetation.

She looked at her phone again. It was already past ten. The hike had taken longer than she'd estimated.

On the return, while climbing over the mess of tree trunks and jutting out limbs and branches again, she grumbled about Tom's idea to place a camera up here.

Why here, out of all the places in the area? If he was out to capture wildlife, he could have instructed her to place the camera off-trail, perhaps closer to a main road so there was less hiking involved. It was possible he didn't want to inadvertently capture images of cows. Where she'd placed the camera was designated wilderness, where cattle weren't allowed. Farther east, ranchers regularly dropped off their cattle in summer to graze the National Forest.

That was one explanation, but she was agitated. There was still something weird about this entire task. She just hoped Tom hadn't sent her out on some wild goose chase and wasn't planning on paying her.

There are a lot of nut cases out there, she thought. *I hope I didn't get sucked in by one.*

The trail camera itself wasn't much collateral in case he flaked on paying her. She'd looked it up online the night before. It was worth a hundred dollars, tops. Still, it was better than nothing.

Maybe he was a retired wildlife biologist who was trying to prove a point to himself. *Possible.*

He did say he used to work for an outfitter and then the county. He hadn't said what he did in that line of work.

Or he wasn't interested in hunting but instead, something to do with elk and sheep migration and climate change. *Less likely.*

Dammit, this is going to bug me.

The downhill hike went much faster, and she half jogged to make up for having lost time in the jackstraw. Once back at her truck, she caught her breath and stretched her legs. She thought of the thrashing her arms and limbs endured, the brutally steep terrain, the overgrown trail, the sketchy creek crossing, and concluded that this was indeed a task for a "rugged" individual with a good four-wheel drive vehicle. Tom was right about that.

No country for old men, she chuckled to herself, thinking of the movie with the same title.

*

She and Sage spent a couple of hours rock climbing later that afternoon before going to a local brewery to get a pizza and chat over a few beers. He was someone she met through a rock climbing and mountaineering Facebook group when she moved to Ridgway two summers prior. He was a couple of years older than she was and also worked multiple part-time jobs in the area to fund his lifestyle. He hung drywall and installed flooring, waited tables sometimes on weekends, and did occasional handyman work. Like her, he rented from a local retired couple who had separate guest quarters adjacent to their main house. It was barely 400 square feet but had southern-facing windows that offered him a view of the green pastures and valley between Ridgway and Ouray.

She enjoyed Sage's relaxed company and sense of humor, but she wasn't attracted to him in a romantic way, which was just as well since he had a girlfriend. She wasn't interested in dating anyway. Relationships were worse than having pets when you're constantly moving, traveling, and going out of town to have new adventures, in her opinion. The last time she was in a relationship was when she lived outside of Tacoma, and the breakup left her questioning what it was she really wanted in life. She didn't want to question that again.

"Can I get a Ska Mexican lager?" Kylar asked the server, a pretty brunette with shoulder-length black hair tinged in purple, her nose studded with a ruby.

"You got it. You?" the server asked Sage.

"Make that two," Sage answered, and added, "and we'll get the spicy artichoke pizza."

The server nodded and left their table to go put in the order. Sage rubbed his face, then scratched his bushy, dark blonde beard with his fingertips. "Man, I'm wiped. I was up at five to get an early start at this drywall job I'm doing so I could be done with plenty of daylight to spare."

"Did you finish?" she asked.

"Not quite. I'll have to go back tomorrow. Pays good, though. I'll be able to pay for that trip to Alberta in July I was telling you about."

"Nice. I'm glad you're still doing that, it sounds like some good mountaineering." She twirled one of the paper coasters on the table. "Yeah, I was up early too for a job. Something new. And strange."

"Yeah, what?"

She explained the basics, then added the punchline. "I get $250 each time, though. Can you believe it?"

"Are you fucking serious?" Sage asked. "Why is some guy paying you that much money to set up a trail camera?"

"Who knows? All I know is that as soon as I was done I emailed him and he Venmo'd me the money right away, so at least I know it's legit."

"Where'd you find out about this job?" He looked over her shoulder and made eye contact with someone in the restaurant, nodded his head slightly in greeting.

"Craigslist. Some dude who lives in Montrose but used to live here," she said. The server arrived with their beers and placed them on the table on top of paper coasters printed with the logo of the brewery. Kylar took a sip of her beer and grunted with pleasure.

Sage high-fived a man that passed their table and exchanged a "what's up" and a few pleasantries before looking back at Kylar. "What's this guy's name?"

"Tom McDougal."

"No way! I know that guy."

"Really? How do you know him?" She leaned in closer. Her long, sun-streaked hair slid from her back over her shoulder and framed her freckled face.

"Well, I don't *know him* know him. I know *of* him. I know his son, Wil. But I don't know Tom personally. He had a reputation when he still lived around here. Used to be quite the character. Would show up to town council meetings, argue with people. He sued a couple of people in town over some business dealings or something." Sage bit his lower lip, looked at his glass, remembering something and chuckled. "I didn't know he still lived around here. Since I hadn't heard about him in a while, I thought he died or something."

"No, he's still alive. And conjuring up odd jobs for locals, apparently." She grinned and took another sip of her beer. "He did seem a bit cantankerous. How do you know his son?"

"Worked with him on some home builds last fall. He's a good guy. Went through a rough divorce, though. I think he did move away, because I haven't seen him since then."

"What else do you know about Tom besides his antagonistic relationship with town council and the residents of Ridgway? What would he pick fights about? What was his deal?"

"Oh, I don't know. He seemed to be against the town spending any money. He was some sort of libertarian or republican or something. Hated tax increases. Whenever there was a proposal for road improvements or affordable housing, he'd be railing against it."

"That's weird," she said. "If he's such a tightwad, how is it that he's willing to fork out so much money to take pictures of animals in the woods?"

"You sure he's interested in animal pictures?"

"What else could it be?"

"Maybe he's got a chip on his shoulder about how many tourists are coming out here and wearing out the trails or something. Like a lot of people around here have, especially ones who move here from bigger cities. They move here because they think it's beautiful, but no one else is allowed to come here because they think it's beautiful. Maybe he's making a case about shutting down the county to outsiders," Sage snorted.

"Weirdo alright." She shook her head and took another sip of her beer. "And anyway, if he was doing that, you'd think he'd pick a more popular trail than the one I was on, like Blue Lakes or something. Doesn't look like anyone goes back where I was this morning."

"You may be right," he acknowledged.

Someone turned up the music that had been playing in the background: a song by Neal Young. A few patrons at the bar cheered and clapped and began singing the lyrics. Kylar and Sage laughed and started singing along, too. Neal resided on a ranch west of Ridgway, so he was a favorite among locals. It wasn't exactly her taste in music, but she liked participating in the fun.

The server returned, this time with their pizza, and Kylar's mouth watered. It'd been a long day with a lot of exertion and time outside, and she was ravenous.

*

On Friday, a week after she set up the trail camera, Kylar returned to retrieve images and to swap out the batteries. It was a cooler day, in the mid-40s when she got into her truck, with a slight breeze coming in from the southwest. She was grateful that there wasn't any wildfire smoke wafting in from Arizona or California and the air was crisp and fresh as snowmelt. Since she already knew the route, she planned to arrive at the trailhead right after first light, giving her ample time to get the job done and then go home, rest a bit, and get cleaned up and ready to work a catering gig she had later that evening in Telluride.

It was the weekend before Memorial Day, and since it had been unseasonably warm all month, she wondered if she'd encounter any campers along the county road at the other trailheads. Despite the pre-dawn darkness, she saw a couple of vehicles parked at the closer trailhead—but no one at the Cow Creek trailhead.

She knew it wasn't a trail that was as promoted as the more popular ones in the area because even she hadn't heard of it until she landed the gig.

She got out of her truck and zipped up her hoodie. A sliver of golden sunlight reflected off the tips of the trees at the top of the mountain across the creek. She smelled the faint scent of woodsmoke and wondered if the campers whose cars she'd seen had gotten up early and were making themselves coffee and breakfast. It was one of her favorite smells, bringing back memories of her childhood: camping with her family in the Cascades, wandering in the woods all day with her two older brothers and the family dog.

She shrugged on her daypack and locked the truck before setting off on the trail. It was still shadowy, but brightening up quickly. She'd brought a headlamp just in case, but she didn't think she would need it.

The switchback section with the downed trees was more arduous than she'd remembered, if that was even possible, and once again she had to refer to the trail map on her phone to find the way across. She hoped that the next location Tom picked for her to hike to after this one was less shaggy.

She arrived at the tree she had selected the previous week and approached the trail camera, tapping on the app that allowed her to connect to it through Bluetooth. After a few seconds, she saw a stack of images appear on her phone. She swiped through a dozen photos and squinted to see what the camera had captured. She noted the time and date stamps.

A deer and two fawns walked past the camera in three frames at 8:43 a.m. the day after she had set up the camera. The fawns were newborns and still polka dotted.

Several photos didn't seem to depict anything. They were taken in the middle of the night at 2:22 a.m. and 3:55 a.m., respectively. The images were dark except where the flash illuminated the grass and low shrubs between the tree trunk and trail. Perhaps a mouse had skittered across the trail but was too small or too hidden to be seen in the image.

Then, a man and a woman with backpacks strode past in four photos. First they faced left, or out toward the longer end of the trail, and then walked past in the opposite direction a few hours later. If they had intended to spend the night, they must have changed their mind. She knew from studying the map before that the trail dead-ended where the creek began, at a waterfall at the edge of a high basin, where snowmelt collected from the tall peaks to the south.

The last photo was taken at 1:12 a.m. that same morning, approximately six hours before she downloaded the images. It showed a large, bulky shape at the bottom of the frame. It appeared to be a big black animal close to the ground with what looked like a tail. A mountain lion? It was hard to tell. The flash had caught its furry backside in a blur of motion.

She replaced the batteries in the camera with fresh ones and made sure the strap was still taught and secure before heading back. She wondered if Tom would make her come back up here to retrieve the camera and reposition it elsewhere, or if he would pay for another week's worth of images. If he decided on the latter, it would cost him $750 for some photos of deer and a couple of hikers. And a blurry photo of a black beast's backside.

"Hey man, whatever floats your boat," she said aloud to the trees. They waved their limbs slightly in the breeze as if raising their arms in response and celebration of the fact that she'd have most of her rent paid after another week of this gig.

*

Minutes after she walked through the door of her apartment, she texted Tom the photos she downloaded and asked him if he was going to keep the camera there another week. He didn't respond at first, and she began to worry that he had come to his senses about his investment in this assignment. But an hour later, after she drank her first cup of coffee that day, he finally texted back.

Thank you for these. Let's keep the camera there for now. I'll send your payment shortly.

She heard the chime of the Venmo notification indicating that Tom had transferred money to her account. She sighed in relief, feeling a little less encumbered. She had made plans to go climbing in the Grenadier Range south of Silverton that weekend with Sage and a couple other friends. Now she could enjoy her time and not worry about picking up more work with the catering company or calling to see if her friend Nancy needed a hand cleaning her clients' Airbnb properties.

Like Sage, she too was trying to save up money for a mountaineering trip. Eventually, she wanted to return to Nepal, but she was also researching a six-day guided excursion in the Chilean Andes to summit the 5,430 meter El Plomo mountain. She'd need at least three thousand dollars for that excursion, which meant that she likely wouldn't be getting there until October at the earliest. She'd need to really hustle this summer and pick up as many gigs as she could.

It was also a relief that, so far, Tom was actually paying her and continuing the assignment. She really wanted to have another conversation with him about what he was doing and why, but she'd wait for the right time to do that. Whatever his answer was, she hoped it took all summer to get whatever data he was after. It was certainly much more pleasant work and more lucrative than scrubbing toilets or serving up hors d'oeuvres to obnoxious rich people in Telluride.

She thought about Tom, living in Montrose, probably with his wife (judging from the family photos and general home décor), conjuring up some cockamamie scheme to monitor hiking trails in the backcountry for a reason that is so important to him that he was willing to generously pay someone to get the job done.

Was he bored? In need of a cause? Wanting to feel relevant and purposeful? She wondered if some people went a little stir-crazy and delusional after retirement. She knew a couple of retired people in town who filled their schedules with so much volunteer work that they were busier after retiring than they ever were when they'd had jobs. Although she also knew many more retirees who filled their time with activities such as travel, visiting their grandkids or playing pickleball, and didn't mind slowing down or relinquishing their status in society.

Tom was used to getting a lot of attention in town, from what Sage told her, so maybe he missed that and was willing to do whatever it took to get it back. That's assuming that his project had anything to do with the community.

She contemplated what it'd be like to be Tom's age and have health issues that prevented her from hiking and climbing. How would she fill her time? Perhaps she'd take up teaching or writing about her mountaineering adventures. Still, the thought of puttering around the house day after day struck her as depressing and claustrophobic.

She didn't like thinking of old age, ill health, and filling the time waiting to die. She was grateful that she could still do everything she wanted to do. Maybe not all the money in the world to do it—yet—but definitely the physical ability and time.

*

A heat wave struck southwest Colorado right after Memorial Day. Kylar suspected that the warmer temperatures would accelerate snow melt in the mountains and send more water downstream, thereby making Cow Creek a bit more challenging to cross. Maybe impossible. She wouldn't know until she got there.

To make matters worse, the morning she embarked on completing the task, the weather changed again and started drizzling. Ominous gray clouds sheared the sky west to east underneath a higher, whiter layer of clouds. She got going right after sunrise in case she would need to go around and hike up and over Stealey Mountain from a different road, which would add about fourteen miles to her 4-mile roundtrip hike to retrieve the images.

Twenty minutes after leaving her apartment, she stopped the truck at the first creek crossing. The flow was definitely higher, but she still wasn't sure if it was going to hinder the truck. Some of the channels were now splashing and overflowing and forming bulbous currents of clear, frigid water. She proceeded, rolling slowly over the rocks and gravel, and looking out the side window as the truck dropped forward into the first channel. It felt solid as it rolled over the choppy terrain and sunk into the creek. Water sloshed heavily and forcefully against the tires and the undercarriage of the truck, making a loud whooshing sound that added to the grinding of the tires against rocks.

It was a bit rough, but passable. Her truck had at least two feet of clearance. At the next creek crossing she had to maneuver around what appeared to be submerged boulders, but managed to get out of the water and up onto the road without incident. Mud puddles started to form on the road, and she had to increase the windshield wiper speed a couple of clicks to be able to see where she was going.

Ugh. It's gonna be a miserable and wet hike today.

She made it to the end of the road and put on her rain gear before getting out of the truck. She'd have to be a bit more nimble today and pick up the pace if she didn't want to spend any more time dealing with the dripping cold. She also was cognizant of the fact that it could start to rain harder, and that meant the creek could surge and trap her on this side of the road.

She tightened the straps of her daypack and jogged up the trail, her breath steady and her energy high. Despite having to be more careful to not slip on the wet and slick jackstraw and injure herself, she covered the two miles to the camera in less than an hour. She downloaded the images under the relatively dry canopy of the tree, changed out the batteries again, and reset the camera. She made sure her phone displayed the images, but she didn't waste too much time examining them. At a glance, the images seemed to have captured a couple more deer and a hiker. She'd examine the photos in more detail once she was back home.

For now, she wanted to get back across the creek before it became impassable.

It occurred to her, as she made her way back, that she would need to return at some point to either retrieve the camera or check it again. Her window of being able to use the same route she was taking to get back was narrowing. If Tom wanted her to move the camera, she might need to return later that day or in the next couple of days at the latest. If he didn't want her to move the camera, she might need to renegotiate her compensation because doing a 20-mile hike to access the location from the other side of Stealey Mountain was going to take her a lot longer than a shortish drive to do a 4-mile hike.

Crap, she thought. *A snag already. I knew this gig was too good to be true.*

She would figure that out later, after she got back home and had cellphone service again.

*

Back home, Kylar changed out of her damp hiking clothes and put the kettle on to make hot tea. The wet weather plunged the outside temperature down into the upper 40s and she had to put the space heater on to cut the chill that had settled into her tiny apartment. She sat down at the worn oak table she'd bought at the second-hand shop in town and reviewed the camera images.

She was right about the deer photos. There was a photo of a mule deer in one shot taken earlier in the week during the heat wave. He was a magnificent 8-point buck that the camera captured as he meandered past. The next day the camera captured a few images of the female deer with her two fawns. Once again, there were several obscure photos taken in the middle of the night. Three photos taken in daylight also appeared to be photos of nothing, until she noticed the brownish shape of chipmunk in one of them, nose to the ground and likely foraging.

Then there were two photos of a hiker. A slender man with a backpack, wearing camouflage-colored pants and a long-sleeved brown or maroon shirt. He appeared to be either in his 20s or 30s, with a head full of rumpled dark brown hair and a scraggly, full beard. His head was down, and he was facing to the right of the frame in the first photo, taken at 8:36 a.m. The next photo was of the same man, this time facing in the opposite direction, at 6:12 p.m.

Something was off about the photos, she thought. What was it?

Kylar reviewed the photos again, but her mind had reached a dead end. She stood up, stretched, and went over to look out the front window of her second-story apartment. Kylar saw her neighbor across the street, kneeling and hunched over, ripping handfuls of grass out of a small flower garden in front of her house. A man who appeared to be in his 60s walked his overweight, spotted cattle dog down the middle of the street. The neighbor woman waved to the man, who then made a right turn and stopped to chat with her while his dog sniffed a nearby tree. A few minutes later, the man yanked the leash and led the dog in the same direction from which he had come.

That's funny, Kylar thought, why did that man decide to go back after speaking to the neighbor lady?

And then it dawned on her. Not about the man, but about what was off about the photos. She walked back to the camera, picked it up off the table, and double-checked the images and the timestamps. When she confirmed they were what she expected, goosebumps bloomed across her arms and scalp.

It was the direction the hiker was facing.

In the first photo in the morning, he was heading toward the trailhead. In the second photo, he was facing the long end of the trail, toward the wilderness boundary. There were no other photos of him.

He came *out* of the wilderness, was gone all day, then returned *back* to the wilderness in the evening two days ago *and hadn't come out again.*

Unless the camera didn't capture his image when it should have, or he went around the camera, or took a different route. Was it possible that he arrived at the trailhead around Memorial Day weekend, spent the night down trail, got back to his vehicle but later remembered that he left something and came back to retrieve it? If that was what happened, why didn't the camera pick up the two additional shots?

Huh. Strange.

She tapped the photos on the phone's screen and magnified them to see if she recognized him or saw any other clues about who he was or what he was doing.

He didn't look familiar. It was hard to tell who he was because she was looking at his profile and his face was obscured by his beard. Sage had a beard that was similar, but he had blond hair, not dark brown hair like the guy in the photo.

There was something else that she noticed.

His backpack. There was something about his backpack.

It was a long, framed pack, something one would take on a multi-night camping trip, with a hip belt and heavy-duty shoulder straps. In the first photo, as he was heading out, the pack appeared empty, a bit flattened in the middle. In the second photo, the one of him heading back in, the pack was bulky and full. She saw that he was subtly more hunched over in the second photo, as if straining under the weight of the pack in a way he wasn't in the first photo.

That doesn't make sense.

She sat, drinking her tea, and pondered what it meant. A few possibilities entered her mind, but knowing what she knew about the drainage up the trail from where she placed the camera and where the trail eventually ended up, she couldn't square these possibilities.

Maybe Tom will have something to say about it, she thought.

She took screen captures of all the images, including the night shots of invisible rodents, and texted them to Tom. She waited until the images went through, then wrote a note:

Hi. Some interesting photos today. I'm wondering what you want to do with the camera because the creek is starting to run higher, and I am not sure I'll be able to cross it with my truck next week. Call me.

She checked her email and looked at Facebook while she waited. Her cellphone rang ten minutes later.

"Hi," Kylar answered, seeing that it was Tom's number that came up on her caller ID.

"Hi Kylar. Thanks for sending me these. So you're saying the creek is running high?" Tom asked.

"Yes, starting to. I mean, I can still get across right now, but I'm not sure for how long. And the problem is that if I can't get across at County Road 12, then I'll have to go around to Owl Creek Pass and hike from the other direction and that—"

"You won't need to do that," Tom said.

"Oh, okay. Good. Because that would be a long day and—"

"Actually, if you can, could you go get the camera and bring it back to me next week? Sounds like you may need to do that soon. I'll pay you for that, of course."

Her stomach dropped. Did she do something wrong? Was he angry with her? He didn't sound angry. He sounded—relaxed, maybe?

"I'm sorry," she said, "I thought you wanted to continue this job throughout the summer. Do you want me to move the camera to a different location, maybe?"

"No, no need. You can bring it back. I'm available Wednesday or Thursday before 10 a.m. When could you do that?"

Kylar's brain seemed to stall. She couldn't recall if she had anything on her schedule the following week. She was supposed to help clean a few rentals next week with Nancy, so she told Tom she'd see him on Thursday.

"I can pay you for today right now or pay you all at once when you return the camera. Which one?" Tom asked.

"All at once is fine," she replied flatly. There was still a part of her that wondered if she was going to get screwed after all.

*

"So my sweet-ass gig is over," Kylar complained to Sage.

"Which one? The trail camera?" he asked as he handed her one of the beers he carried from the refrigerator and went to sit down on the futon couch next to his girlfriend, Shannon.

"Yep," Kylar said and made a pouty face.

"Why? What happened?" Sage asked.

"I don't know. I've been thinking about it all day. I wonder if he got annoyed at me for saying that I wouldn't be able to cross the creek soon because of the water flow. I mean, he did make it a point to say he wanted a 'rugged' individual with a good vehicle.

Maybe he's going to find someone more qualified to risk crossing a rushing river. Or maybe he thinks I should swim across when the time comes."

"You have a job where you're crossing a creek?" Shannon asked and then stretched her arm across the back of the couch and started to play with Sage's hair.

"Yeah, crossing a creek and hiking a few miles to download pictures from a trail camera," Kylar said. "Apparently I'm not the 'man' for the job."

Sage gave Kylar a dubious look.

"Well, it's true!" Kylar grumbled.

"Is that what he told you?" Sage asked.

Kylar shook her head and took a sip of her beer. She let out a long, exasperated sigh.

"Well, then tell me what happened today," said Sage. "Let's figure this out."

She explained the situation, including her assessment of the rising waters of the creek and the possibility of having to hike up and over the mountain and spend all day doing it next time.

"What about the pictures you got off the camera?" asked Shannon. "Was there something in them that made this guy decide he didn't need you babysitting the camera anymore?"

Kylar opened her mouth to dismiss the idea, then stopped. Of course! She didn't just get photos of deer and mice. "You know, Shannon, it could be. I did get some shots of people. In fact, there was one guy in the photos that looked like he was coming off the trail and then returning to it later. Strange, like where was he going, ya know?"

Sage leaned forward toward Kylar. "You have those photos on your phone? Let me see them."

Kylar reached into her daypack, which she had dropped on the side of the chair when she arrived at Sage's apartment, removed her phone, swiped her finger across the screen a few times, and handed the phone to him. "You can see the whole group of pictures there if you swipe through."

He furrowed his brow as he examined each photo briefly. Then he paused, brought the phone closer to his face, and made a gesture with his fingers to magnify an image. "Holyyyyy shit, Kylar."

"What? What!" She got up off the chair and came around to see what he was looking at. It was the photo of the scruffy hiker with the backpack. Sage pointed to the photo and then looked up at her, his eyes wide, his mouth a small O.

"This guy. It's Wil. Wilmore McDougal."

Kylar shook her head to indicate she didn't get it.

"Tom McDougal's son."

Oh. Kylar stood up straight and looked at Sage, then Shannon, then back at Sage. "You're kidding. You recognize him?"

"It's him," said Sage. "I recognize the red backpack, too, from when we went camping with him and his wife once." He showed the photo to Shannon, who nodded in agreement.

"What's he doing out there? Camping? By himself?" Kylar shook her head, still trying to reconcile what she knew about Tom, his "personal project" and this discovery.

"Maybe," he said. "And maybe Tom is paying you to spy on him for some reason."

"Spy on him? What for?" She took her phone back from Sage and sat back down in the chair. "That's weird."

"Well yeah it's weird. He's a weirdo, I told you," he said. "Anyway, you should ask him. Tom, I mean."

She thought for a minute. She needed to remove the camera soon, and then go to Tom's house to return it to him. That would be a good opportunity to confront him with what she knew. He would have to explain things, wouldn't he? Especially if she flat out told him she knew that he had paid her to get photos of his son.

She picked her beer bottle up from the coffee table and fingered the paper label, scratching a corner of it until it started to peel back. She felt lighter. Relieved, in a way. Yes, the gig may be over, but at least it wasn't because she was incompetent or incapable of performing it.

*

The first chance she had to go back to the camera was the following Wednesday. The creek looked marginally higher, but was still passable, thanks to temperatures coming back down to the low to mid-70s. She didn't bother downloading the images to her phone since she was returning the entire unit to Tom the next day. She did, however, examine the images that had been generated since the previous Friday when she had cleared the cache.

There he was again. The man that Sage thought was Wil.

The photo was taken the day before, on a Tuesday. Again, on a Tuesday, he had walked past the camera in the direction of the trailhead in the morning and then returned back toward the forest and canyon later that afternoon. Just like the week before, his backpack looked heavier and fuller in the second photo.

He's not randomly going hiking. He's getting supplies and bringing them back.

But where had he been going, and how was he getting there? There was no car at the trailhead that she recalled seeing. At least, not at the Cow Creek trailhead. Was his car elsewhere along the side of the road that she hadn't noticed? She'd have to see if she noticed any parked cars on her drive back. Also, wouldn't he worry about being trapped on this side of the creek soon?

Unless he wasn't crossing the creek.

Unless he was climbing up and over Stealey Mountain and ending up on the other side, at the eastern trailhead. But why would he do that? It was at least a 9-mile hike one way from the location of the camera, perhaps longer, depending on where he was coming from.

She stuffed the camera into her daypack and made her way back to the trailhead and her truck, looking forward to unraveling this mystery soon.

*

Kylar drove to Montrose to return the camera to Tom the next day. She pondered how she would bring up the issue of the man in the photos. Should she ask Tom directly? Should she say she thinks it's his son, or would that make it glaringly obvious that she was discussing her assignment with others? She was fairly certain Tom wouldn't approve of that.

For sure she wanted to know why Tom abruptly cut the assignment short. She suspected it was because he had proof that his son was camping back in the wilderness off the Cow Creek drainage, but she still had nagging thoughts that he didn't think she was up for the job.

She parked in the driveway, walked up to his front door, and rang the bell, camera in hand. She'd waited just a few seconds when a woman opened the door. She looked to be in her 60s, with very short gray hair and a slightly hunched posture that rounded her shoulders and made her look frail. She looked at Kylar with a tinge of concern before her face softened in some sort of recognition.

"Hi, you must be here for Tom. Come in, he's in the backyard. I'll go get him." The woman stepped aside, motioning Kylar into the foyer. Kylar opted to stay on the tile floor as opposed to taking her shoes off to step onto the carpet like she did the first time. Even though she hadn't introduced herself, she assumed the woman was Tom's wife.

Kylar watched her disappear toward the back of the house where the kitchen was, where she had first discussed the job with Tom. Next to the entry, where she stood now, was a sitting room with a dark blue upholstered couch underneath a bay window and two formal chairs facing the couch with what looked to be a lacquered wooden table in between. Behind that was a formal dining room with a hutch, filled with ornate dinnerware and knick-knacks. It was all very old fashioned and formal, in her opinion. In contrast, her taste ran minimalist and second-hand store cheap.

Tom appeared a minute later, his face faintly pink from the sun, a slight smile on his face. Kylar extended her hand to pass him the camera. He took it without looking at it and looked at her instead.

"There are more pictures on there from the last few days," she offered. She nervously cleared her throat before continuing. "Umm. In case you're interested."

"Ok, thanks for bringing this back. I appreciate that I've been able to rely on you," Tom said.

She shifted her weight to her other foot and put her hands in the pockets of her hiking pants. "I'm just wondering why you're done with the camera. Was it something I did or didn't do?"

He narrowed his eyes. "No, nothing to do with you. I just got what I needed, and a lot sooner than I expected."

"Which was what, may I ask?" Her voice didn't sound as confident as she would have liked. Although his statement made her feel better, she still didn't want to leave without knowing what the story was with the camera and his son. She was still afraid he would see her question as unnecessarily nosy and ask her to leave.

He let out a long sigh, then looked down at the carpet, as if contemplating just how much to tell her. "Well," he started, "you see, our son's been missing for six months. We hadn't heard from him at all since Thanksgiving of last year, which is the last time we saw him. We weren't sure what happened to him and would have reported him missing, but apparently he'd cleared out his bank account and told his wife he was going to be gone for a while. So Gayle—my wife—and I knew he was somewhere, we just didn't know where."

Kylar feigned surprise. "Oh. So that's who was in the photo the camera took? The man with the beard and backpack?"

"Yes. That's him."

"I don't understand. How did you know he'd be out there? And aren't you worried about him?" she asked.

"My son has mental health issues, Kylar," he said, his voice lowering a pitch. "But are we worried about him? Yes and no. I know he's a capable person out in the wilderness. So in that sense, I think he's okay. We're just not sure what his state of mind is."

"But wait a minute, are you saying he's been missing since last Thanksgiving? And living out there by himself?" Her jaw dropped. Back in that remote, craggy backcountry, *in the winter?*

"I don't know. Maybe. Or somewhere. I just remember him telling me once that that was his favorite place to go backpacking and hunting because not many people go back there. That's why I suspected that if he was roughing it somewhere nearby, that place was a good contender."

Her mind raced. How could anyone live back there, without access to shelter or food or a vehicle? Where had he been going the last two Tuesdays when the camera caught him leaving the area?

"Is your son some kind of survivalist or something?" she asked, still dumbfounded.

"I wouldn't say survivalist. When we lived in Alaska, he learned a lot from me about building a shelter, hunting, and foraging. He and his sister loved to camp and explore and even built a small cabin-like shelter on our property, which they'd used as a club-house when their friends came over." He looked down at the camera he was holding in his hand. "He's skilled in the outdoors, and he used to talk about finding a place in the mountains where he could buy a piece of property and build a house like we had in Alaska."

Tom stopped talking and looked down at his hands. "Anyway, I was going on a hunch, since there was no sign of him using his credit cards or his social security number or his cellphone in months. We just needed to know he was ok. That he was still alive. Turns out that he is."

Kylar nodded, processing what she'd heard, and waited for Tom to say more. When he didn't, she added, "I'm sorry to hear you've been going through this. It must be hard."

He looked off to the side, his lips pursed, his eyes glassy.

"Is there anything else I can do to help?" she asked, suddenly aware that he might interpret her question as asking for more work, which wasn't her intention.

"No," he answered flatly. "In fact, I'd appreciate it if you kept this to yourself. It's a personal matter between me and my family."

"Of course," she said sheepishly, knowing she'd tell Sage everything later if and when he asked. "If there is anything you need, just give me a call, Tom."

He thanked her and opened the front door, signaling the visit was over and there was nothing more to be said. Before he shut the door behind her, he told her he'd send her the last payment later that day. She walked slowly back to the truck, relieved but befuddled.

*

"Mental health issues? What the fuck? Wil doesn't have mental health issues," Sage scoffed.

Kylar had texted Sage on her way back home from Tom's house, eager to get his take on what she'd just learned. He invited her to meet him at a home construction site where he was working at hanging drywall. When she arrived, she found him inside, dressed in painter's overalls, taping panels. There were two more guys at the other end of the house, working at something in the kitchen. She could hear chatting and the sound of drilling, and the occasional *whap whap* of a nailgun.

She pulled up an empty orange Home Depot bucket, flipped it upside down, and sat down. "That's what he seems to believe. Maybe he's right. Who in their right mind is going to go live in the woods, *over winter, in the mountains*, for no good reason?"

"Nah, that's bullshit. Something else is going on." Sage trimmed a piece of tape off with a utility knife he had in his back pocket.

"Well, hang on. How well do you know Wil? I mean, people have all kinds of shit going on in their head that most people are not aware of."

"I know he's not a lunatic."

"And you know this for a fact?"

"I mean, he's not my BFF or anything, but I've worked with him, and we hung out once in a while, went backpacking that one time. He strikes me as a solid guy. We'd have fairly normal conversations about fairly normal things." He moved the ladder he was using down a few feet and stepped up a couple rungs to tape a seam close to the ceiling.

"So what's your theory? About why he's checked out and living in the woods?"

"How do we know he's living up there? Maybe he's just camping. Maybe he lives somewhere else."

Kylar bit her lip and thought for a minute. Tom didn't say why he was so sure; she'd just assumed that he had exhausted other theories and possibilities. She'd assumed from what he'd said that he must have hired an investigator to find him.

"If he was living somewhere else," she said, "I think Tom would have found out. He seemed very motivated to know Wil's whereabouts."

"Good point," he murmured.

"Don't you want to find out?"

"Find out?"

"About what he's doing up there and why? I mean, he *is* your friend. Or was."

"Sounds to me like you're the one who wants to find out." He stepped back down to the floor and turned around to face her. "But yeah, I guess I am wondering if he's okay. What? You have a funny look on your face."

Kylar blinked and then took out her cellphone and tapped the screen and swiped a few times. "What are you doing next Monday?"

"I don't know. Working, probably. Why?"

"You want to go on a little overnight camping trip with me? Up to the trailhead. Probably over Stealey Mountain, though. By then the creek will be too high to drive across."

"You think you're going to find him up there?"

"Hopefully. I think he leaves on Tuesdays to re-supply or something, so I bet we can intercept him in the morning before he gets too far. I'm dying to know how he's getting into town, too. There's no vehicle parked at the trailhead." She looked up at Sage, wide-eyed, her smile mischievous. "We can leave after you're done with work if you want. It won't take us long to get there, pitch a tent. What do you say?"

Sage nodded. "Ok. Sure. Let's do it. Let's find out what ol' Wil is up to. If nothing else, even if we don't run into him, I'll get to hike a trail I haven't done yet."

"That's the spirit!" she exclaimed, slapping her knee.

*

It was a warm evening when Kylar and Sage started their trek across the mountain to find Wil.

She had spent the day climbing near Telluride and was feeling a bit of fatigue from the heat and sun, but the prospect of a sunset hike and spending a night under the stars invigorated her again. She'd packed enough food to have a small meal before they turned in for the night, and something for breakfast the next morning. They planned to wake before sunrise so they didn't miss their chance to intercept Wil. If all went according to plan, they'd be back at her truck by mid-morning the next day. Sage had to get to work by noon at the latest, as did she, because she wanted to pick up a couple of vacation rental cleanings.

The sun shone golden rays through the canopy of quivering aspen leaves on the first half of their hike. Then, as they ascended higher up the mountain, she was treated to expansive views of the lush green pastures at the bottom of the valley. Rounding the mountain, she kept glancing to the south through pine trees at the tall peaks of the Sneffels Range. The route was overgrown with grass and low shrubs. It was muddy in places where rainwater had pooled from a brief thunderstorm a few days before. By the time they arrived at the highest point of the trail, the sun was low and blanketing the western horizon in orange and pink. She got out her headlamp and Sage followed suit.

Back at the bottom of the mountain, they joined up to the road that she had driven to get to the trailhead, walked another quarter of a mile, and started to discuss where to pitch their tents. She wanted to be as inconspicuous as possible but still be able to see anyone who'd come out of the forest and onto the road. They found a good flat spot between the road and the creek, which was as wide and deep as she'd seen it, sloshing over boulders and splashing its way downhill.

After filtering some water and cooking it over a compact camp stove that Sage brought, they made some tea to go with their sandwiches and chips. They sat on a log and talked until fatigue overtook her and she crawled into her tent and sleeping bag and stretched her limbs before falling into a deep, delicious sleep.

*

Kylar's phone's alarm went off right before sunrise. She couldn't believe it was morning already. It was as if she'd been knocked unconscious the moment her head hit the camp pillow. She didn't remember even shifting around in her bag.

She guessed they'd have enough time to at least make some coffee and eat something before Wil made his way down. If he was even coming down that day. Her theory about his schedule was just that: a theory. It could have been a coincidence that he passed by the trail camera two Tuesdays in a row.

The water started boiling in the pan by the time Sage emerged from his tent, and she set out two metal mugs and scooped out some instant coffee into each one.

"Hey."

"Hey. How'd you sleep?" she asked him.

"Like the dead. I was tired. Still tired, actually."

She handed him the mug of steaming coffee, then unpacked the items she'd brought for them to share out of her backpack. There were a half dozen hardboiled eggs, a loaf of banana bread she'd made, and two apples.

"What are you going to say when you see him?" she asked.

Sage shrugged. "'What are you doing out here, bro?'"

"Don't tell him how we know he's here. Pretend that we're just, you know, doing a little camping trip."

"You don't think he'll think it's bizarre that we're camped out here off the road, right at the trailhead?"

She bit into the egg she'd peeled. "Mmm, I think he'll be too shocked to see you to think much of it."

They sat in silence, eating and listening to the rush of the creek and the chickadees singing in the trees above and behind them. The sun shined on the top half of the mountain across the water, exposing the craggy rock formations and clumps of evergreen. She brushed some rocks and gravel off the ground and lay down flat on her back, looking up at the clear sky and smelling the air. She reveled in how wild and isolated this place felt, now that the road was cut off. They hadn't run into anyone since they arrived at the trailhead on the other side of the mountain.

She closed her eyes and was almost dozing when Sage nudged her with his foot.

"Wha—?" she grumbled and squinted at him. He tilted his head, signaling for her to look at what he was seeing.

A man with a backpack was walking towards them from the Cow Creek trail. He was still far enough away that she couldn't make out his features, but she was sure this was Wil. Same stature, same clothes, same beard.

"Is that him?" she whispered.

"Can't tell yet. Act chill."

She sat up and brushed the dirt off her back and shoulders, then turned toward the road. Sage was already on his feet, hands in his pant pockets, facing the man, who'd spotted them and was looking in their direction. He maintained his pace and locked eyes with Sage.

As the man approached within fifty feet of them, Sage broke the silence. "Wil? Is that you?"

The man slowed and then stopped, staring at Sage with a wary expression. He was now within ten feet of them. Kylar hugged her knees but remained seated on the ground.

"It's Sage," Sage said.

Wil's expression changed; his lips parted slightly, and he furrowed his brow.

"Sage?" Will said, hesitating.

"Yeah, dude! What the heck running into you here?"

Sage was doing a good job acting surprised and delighted, Kylar thought. She tried to keep her expression neutral since she technically wasn't supposed to know Wil.

"What are you doing here?" asked Wil, his posture suddenly rigid.

"My friend Kylar and I are doing a little backpack. What are you doing?"

Wil looked at her then back at Sage. He didn't answer right away, and she looked up at Sage, who, to his credit, continued to smile at Wil and wait for his response.

"Yeah, I was backpacking, too," said Wil, his tone hesitant and careful. "Heading back today."

"Where's your car, man?" Sage asked. "Hopefully not on this road because you won't get over the creek."

Wil looked back toward the trailhead and up back at Sage. "Where's *your* car?" He asked, his tone dry and challenging.

"We parked on the other side of Stealey, hiked up and over. Is that where you're going?"

Wil stared at Sage for a few seconds, then turned and started walking away in a brisk pace. Sage glanced over at Kylar and shook his head, then jogged to catch up with Wil. He shouted to Wil to hold up and maneuvered his way in front of him while walking backward. The two men started speaking loudly to each other. She made out only a few words, mostly expletives. Then Sage approached closer to Wil and spoke quietly to him, his head hung in a conspiratorial posture. After a few minutes, Wil's shoulders slumped slightly, and he put his hands in the pockets of his camo pants.

They stood talking like that for what seemed like several minutes, then Sage touched Wil's shoulder and walked slowly back to where she sat waiting. They watched as Wil walked down the road and up the Stealey trailhead, where he turned and disappeared into the trees.

She waited patiently but her patience ran out after a minute. "Well, what the fuck did he say?!"

Sage sat down in front of her. "He didn't buy the 'oh, we're just backpacking' story. He accused us of spying on him. So I told him about your gig and how we knew he was here."

"Oh shit, no, Sage!"

"Sorry. I didn't think he was going to believe anything else. Anyway, he said he was going into town for supplies, like you thought, and that he had a motorbike stashed under a tarp on the other side of the mountain somewhere."

"So that's how he's getting in and out. Did he say anything else? Is he squatting out here? Was he here all last winter and spring?"

"Sounds like it. I asked him if he was okay and if he needed anything and he said he loved it out here and just wanted to be left alone. When I mentioned how we knew he was out here, about the camera and Tom and all that, he flipped out. Said, and I quote, *that man is a monster*. And then begged me to not say anything to Tom about us running into him. He wouldn't tell me any more than that. He was very insistent, though. Seemed really worried about Tom finding him here."

"Too late for that."

"True, but based on what you told me, he can't really hike his way over here on his own, can he?"

"No."

They started to pack up their tents and put their gear into their packs. She thought about what must have happened with Wil to make him decide to bug out into the wilderness. She wondered if what Tom said about Wil having mental health issues was true, and if so, what that meant for Wil's survival out here. How long would he hide out like this? He must have been skilled at building a shelter and perhaps even hunting and foraging, but there was a limit to how long a person could do that and thrive— wasn't there?

"He must be going somewhere where he knows no one will recognize him when he goes in for food and stuff," Sage said. "Because I sure as hell haven't seen him around the grocery store. Not in Ridgway, not in Montrose. And apparently his parents haven't seen him, either."

They looked around their campsite to make sure they got everything and then started walking back to the trail, now at least fifteen minutes behind Wil.

"He's probably going to the Walmart in Delta or something," she guessed. Delta was another twenty miles north of Montrose and it wasn't likely that Tom would run into Wil there.

They continued to talk about what had transpired, in an attempt to unravel Wil's strange situation. But the more they talked about it, the more questions they had. Was someone helping Wil? Did this have to do with money? Was Wil in trouble with the law? Did his ex-wife know where he was? Was he hiding from her, too?

Was he even hiding?

Before they got back to her truck, she noticed single tire tracks leading out of the woods and out to the narrow road that led to the trail parking area, about the size of a motorcycle tire. She pointed it out to Sage, who said he didn't notice them before, and they looked fresh. They looked up into the forest above—mostly tall, mature aspens with an understory of ferns and 4-foot-tall fledgling aspens. It was difficult to tell from where the tracks had originated, but she imagined that it would probably not be that difficult to hide a small motorcycle under a green or brown tarp in the boscage.

"Wow. Incredible that Wil has managed to survive out there for so many months—in the winter, no less. Did you know that your friend was such a badass?" she asked, as they drove down the hill toward Ridgway.

"No more of a badass than anyone else I know," he replied and smiled at her. "Although, I'm not sure that what he's doing is bad-assery or fuckery. Or just nuts."

"What looks nuts to some can be the only sane thing to do for others," said Kylar, thinking of Wil, but also thinking of her own estrangement from her parents, and the path her life had taken since she'd seen them last.

*

Three days later, shortly after sunrise, a thin plume of light gray smoke drifted up from the Cow Creek drainage and quickly became a thick dark cloud that billowed between the mountains and rolled out west onto the valley below the Cimarron Range. Kylar had gone paddleboarding with a friend in the state park that morning, and they watched the wildfire almost double in size in the short time they were in the reservoir. She didn't mention her gig or Wil or her and Sage's trek to find him.

She didn't share her concern that there was a man in that general area who may be trapped and in danger.

As soon as she got back to her apartment and was alone, however, she called Sage to ask him what they should do, knowing that the fire looked to be located in the same drainage where Wil had his encampment. She had read on social media that several wildfire teams had already been dispatched to the area, including the Ridgway volunteer fire department. He suggested they could call the fire department with an anonymous tip and let them take it from there. She agreed, and he offered to be the one to make the call.

The fire burned two thousand acres by the time the monsoonal flow arrived—unusually early— and dampened the fire with two days of rain and thunderstorms.

The local paper related that there had been a report of a missing hiker in the area, but that crews couldn't locate him due to the remote location and the danger posed by the fire itself.

A month after the fire started, it was contained enough that investigators could go in and look for evidence of how it started and whether the missing hiker had perished. They didn't find a body, but the investigators did find evidence of a "small log structure" that had been charred, although it wasn't determined that that was where the fire originated.

Kylar never heard from Tom again, nor had she or Sage spotted Wil in town or anywhere else since they'd intercepted him on the trail.

Wil had either escaped the fire and relocated, or had gotten trapped and died in it.

*

Kylar thought about Wil often in the months that followed, with a mix of melancholy and reverence. Here was a man who had not only decided that he wanted to escape into the wilderness but had the balls and the skills to do it and survive—at least for many months, during the harshest time of the year. Whether or not it had been a good idea or had resulted in accidental destruction of a swath of wilderness, or his own destruction, she wasn't sure. Wil may have been the one who started the fire, or it could have been other campers in the area to blame.

She also wondered if Wil had set the fire intentionally, to shake his father off his trail and make him believe he had died. If that were the case, he must have had a very good reason to not want to be found. Or maybe Tom had been right and he was suffering from delusions or whatever else.

Later that year, in November, as she was making the trek up to basecamp to climb El Plomo in Chile, she again thought about Wil and wondered if maybe there was a subset of people who just weren't meant to thrive in modern society. Maybe they felt crushed by purposeless or demeaning work, crushed by the mercilessness of debtors or shitty bosses, demoralized by the spiral of worsening environmental problems, and helpless in the face of it all.

Maybe they were wounded by trauma, unable to escape the onslaught of painful memories and negative self-talk.

Maybe the only thing that gave these people respite from the immutable expectations of society or family was complete immersion in the beauty and solitude of wilderness, or the perceived benevolence of nature.

She knew that nature wasn't benevolent any more than humankind was benevolent. To thrive *in* this world, you have to be *of* this world: sensitive enough to appreciate the splendor but resilient and strong enough to survive the brutality.

On the way to the summit, she and the rest of the expedition group passed an ancient and weathered cluster of massive, carved stones that were arranged into a wall. The guide explained that it was a ceremonial structure built five hundred years ago by the Incas, and that a young boy's mummified body had been discovered there. The boy's elaborate garb indicated that he had been sacrificed in a ritual, which likely began with a several-day procession up to the mountain and ended with him being buried beneath a layer of flagstones in a frozen tomb.

When she heard this, she shuddered, imagining both the terror the boy must have felt, along with the electrifying anticipation of transcendence. Had he understood the magnitude of the sacrifice he was making for his tribe? Was he told there was eternal love and beauty on the other side of his suffering?

She followed the group up the mountain, eventually conceding that some questions may never be answered, and the motivations of some tortured souls would always remain a mystery.

A NOTE FROM THE AUTHOR

Mountains captivate our imagination and allude to the experience of adventure and spiritual transcendence. They entice us to walk their shadowy canyons and cross their secret meadows, and we yearn to answer their call.

To live surrounded by mountains can feel like a spiritual experience for some. I know it does for me.

But there's a paradox between what some might imagine is the dream of living in the mountains and the reality of it.

In a small mountain town, there's more intimacy with people in the community because there are fewer people. Fewer people means you have to make more of an effort to find your "tribe", and you can hardly afford to alienate yourself from your neighbors. There's silence and solitude, but that can feel isolating. There's a rare and intense natural beauty, but that means real estate is in demand and expensive. Jobs are scarce and high-paying jobs are even scarcer. If you live here, you have to bring your job (or your retirement savings) with you or work multiple low-paying jobs to make ends meet. Some who relocate to the mountains from the city have had to move back because of financial stress.

Sometimes, these realities can create unforeseen challenges and have stressful effects on the psyche. It can trigger an existential crisis for some.

A National Geographic blog by Kelley McMillan written in 2016 about the mental health crisis in small mountain towns like Telluride declares, "These idyllic locales breed a particular kind of malaise." Yes, living in the mountains can be "living the dream" for some. For others, it can lead to depression and sometimes suicide, as the article reports.

In this collection of fictional stories I explored this paradox between the captivation of mountains and the demands of living in a place that—by nature—can be socially isolating, financially stressful, and emotionally demanding. These stories are born of my imagination and the characters are not based on anyone I know personally.

Missing is a fictional story that was inspired by a real event, when a woman mysteriously went missing and was found far from town in the wilderness of the Uncompahgre Plateau. When I followed this story, I wondered what really happened and why that woman ended up where she did. This led me to creating the fictional account of Judy. But *Missing* isn't just an account of a missing person, but also an examination of what can go missing from a marriage that can lead a person to feel so completely alone. It's also a comment on what happens when life plans are shattered by unforeseen or unexpected circumstances.

Retreat is about a man who believes that all that's needed to enable him to finally relax and change his workaholic ways is to spend a couple of weeks in the cliché of a "cabin in the woods". What he doesn't know is that nature and solitude can have a strange effect on an uninitiated mind. Having studied ecopsychology, I know the many ways in which spending time in nature can be healing and life changing. However, it can also bring up unpleasant feelings and past trauma. Once the distractions of modern life fall away, we are left to face ourselves, which can be either a relief or a terror, or both.

Dog explores one of the annoyances of living in mountain ranch country: people don't always fence in their dogs. *Dog* depicts a widow's extreme response to a misunderstanding about her neighbor and his wandering dog. A psychological battle ensues between Bev and Bones. Bones represents chaos, the problem that we can't control and can't foresee. Bones is the mosquito that ruins the perfect picnic. In her desperation to control her mosquito—her Bones—Bev ends up pulling her dream life into a nightmare and possibly becoming the town crazy woman, that single widow that once kidnapped her neighbor's dog.

Gig was inspired by an actual Craigslist ad I read that I couldn't stop thinking about (but never investigated). It presents an improbable assignment offered to a woman who represents the kind of rugged, idealist adventurers who reside in mountain towns. The gig itself is beside the point. A much bigger question is presented to you, the reader: what happens when a person equates being in nature with inherent freedom? Can one avoid conforming to society's expectations of personal success and "living a good life" without losing something in return? What is lost when one chooses to live a life outside what others would consider "normal"?

I present these stories as cautionary tales of what living in a small mountain town entails. These are just meant to convey that while it takes a certain kind of individual who would even *want* to live in a small, mountain town, it also takes a certain kind of individual to be able to successfully *adapt* to it.

For those who've made the choice to reside here on the boundary of civilization and wilderness, I commend you. I know from personal experience that, while it may have felt like the obvious choice to move here, it's not an easy choice. But once the mountains settle deep into your heart, it's hard to imagine any other place you'd rather be.

ABOUT THE AUTHOR

Margaret Emerson holds a master's degree in Ecopsychology and has written hundreds of self-help and relationship advice articles for psycho-therapists, coaches, and personal development experts through her work as a ghostwriter and marketing copywriter. She's also the author of *Contemplative Hiking Along the Colorado Front Range.* She resides on a homestead in Ridgway, Colorado with her husband and enjoys hiking, fishing, and gardening.

Visit her website, www.RidgwayWritingWorkshops.com for information on current classes and writing retreats.

www.ingramcontent.com/pod-product-compliance
Lightning Source LLC
Chambersburg PA
CBHW070608120726
47909CB00007B/2496